HOW WOMEN WILL CHANGE THE WORLD

How Women Will Change the World

The Journey Continues

THE GIFTED ONE ~ BOOK II

Andy McCabe

City Bear Press
Manahawkin, NJ

SYNOPSIS

THE GIFTED ONE
BOOK I

The Journey Begins

The protagonist is a down-and-out writer who is mentally, physically, and spiritually bankrupt. By coincidence, he meets a messenger disguised as a homeless man and is asked to commit a random act of kindness. The reward for his assistance is a book and card explaining that he has been chosen to help change the world; however, to do so, he must commit to changing himself by spending one week at the training camp of a reclusive and mysterious man who seems partly mythical.

In a leap of faith, the writer goes to an isolated ranch in Arizona. Here, he meets a Native American woman who captures his heart. The week is full of lessons and truths that make us realize how our lives can become what we want them to be—if we follow the guidelines presented.

On the final day of this transformative week, the writer is given a mission by his mentor, the Gifted One, who prefers to call himself "Coach." His mission is to make the changes in himself that will become the foundation for his work in bringing about changes in the world.

Cover design by Nathaniel Sharkey
Book design by Lynn Else
Publishing logo design by Steve Zazenski

Library of Congress Library of Congress Control Number is 2016939168

ISBN 978-0-692-79111-0 (paperback)
ISBN 978-1-945173-36-3 (e-book)

Published by City Bear Press
19 Henry Drive
Manahawkin, NJ 08050

www.citybearpress.com

Printed and bound in the
United States of America

DEDICATION

To Dr. Peter Kalellis
psychologist, author, and dear friend
who introduced me to Sappho and traveled with me to
the Greek island of Lesbos, his birthplace.

"If there ever comes a time when the women of the world come together purely and simply for the benefit of mankind, it will be a force such as the world has never known."

—Matthew Arnold
Nineteenth-century poet and philosopher

CONTENTS

PREFACE

In presenting a story, which, although seemingly improbable, could very well be true, it is my hope that it will remind women of their power.

Why women and why now? Most folks, who are paying even the slightest attention, would agree that the world is in a mess and most of the chaos and pending calamity has been caused by men. Men control the world and, mostly, always have.

Tony Montana summed it up in the 1983 movie, *Scarface*, which I have watched more times than I care to admit, when he said, "In this country, you gotta make the money first. Then when you get the money, you get the power. Then when you get the power, then you get the women."

But there's more! The aggression hormone: testosterone. Going back beyond recorded history, you can always bet that the guy who controlled things was as aggressive as hell. He didn't take a vote. He beat someone in a fight or killed them and that's it. He called the shots! Sound familiar? Consider, for example, Julius Caesar, Attila the Hun, Vikings, Hitler, and on and on.

However, now men don't have to beat someone in a fight, they only need to have unlimited money and then they can buy power and, if needed, someone to do their fighting for them. But it's still about women! All the "power" boys want to impress the ladies, and it usually works. Many women will agree that the more powerful and wealthy a man is, the more attractive he seems to get!

For women, on the other hand, beauty has always been the characteristic that has attracted men. It still is. However, most women don't seek power for the same reasons as men. They generally don't do it to get the best looking guy. Women are overwhelmingly more interested in family, social issues, correcting wrongs, making a difference, taking care of others and taking care of their loved ones, as well our planet. Sure, there are women who don't fit this template, but most, in the opinion of this humble writer, do! Women don't want to send their young men to war, regardless of the reason. If women where in charge, I believe we wouldn't have wars.

So, we live in a world controlled by wealthy men who pull the strings on everything: media, politics, war, money, education, food, medicine, wages, jail, and now, your mind. They've been at it for a long time. Now, they control your mind by making you afraid. Afraid? Think about it: the Ebola epidemic, swine influenza, nuclear annihilation, uncontrolled spending, a faltering economy, downsizing, mandated vaccinations, a government out of control, possible food and water shortages, climate change, terrorism, and scariest of all, WW III. What is insulting is that, even when the medical profession knows the flu vaccine often doesn't work, the signs are still out at most pharmacies reminding us to get our flu shots now. No appointment needed!

In 2009, the Dalai Lama stated, "Western women will save the world!"[1] I believe him. He obviously doesn't fit the money, power, women mold, and his life has been spent in service to others. He has also never capitulated to his enemies, but instead, serves as a beacon for perseverance, strength, and enlightenment. It is my wish and prayer that this book will make a difference by reminding women of their power and challenging them to do what needs to be done to ensure the well-being of future generations.

This is not a book that tries, in any way, to portray women as saints and men as sinners. Each camp has its share. There are, obviously, many great men and women and lots of folks in between. This is also not a book that purports women should rule the world. This is a book about balance: the yin and yang, the up and down, night

1 Dalai Lama, Vancouver Peace Summit, October 2009. See: http://dalailamacenter.org/blog-post/western-women-can-come-rescue-world.

and day, male and female. Currently, there is no balance, and therein rests much of the problem.

When women fully appreciate their power, they will make needed changes in themselves, their family, community, workplace, politics, and the world.

Regarding politics, which affects us all, when electing our leaders, I suggest that we carefully review their track record before electing someone. That's what most of us do before we place our bet on a horse race. In making decisions about leaders and whether they should be men or women, asking the following questions will help clarify the process: Do they have a record of sincerity? Do they have a record of being successful at what they do? Are they compassionate and kind? Do they know how to get things done? Do they really care about people? Do you believe they would use their power with restraint but, when necessary, for the good of our country and the world? Most importantly, do they have a record of being truthful and honest?

Many of our leaders in the United States are interested only in promoting the companies and nations who donate to their campaign and not in the general welfare of the citizens and the world.

INTRODUCTION

On a windswept and rainy day over two thousand five hundred years ago, a girl was born on the Greek island of Lesbos. Her birth had been predicted long before by the Oracle at Delphi, who had foretold that one day, after more than two millennia had passed, she would reincarnate and play a major role in healing the world.

Her parents were uneducated and poor. However, before her birth, her father had a dream where he saw a baby girl writing down the thoughts of a scholarly woman. At that time in Greece, girls were not educated; only boys were afforded the privilege. After the child's birth, the wind and rain stopped, and the air became pure with a clean scent. The mother and father decided they would call her Katerina, a Greek name meaning pure.

Years later, the father became the caretaker for a school for girls. It was the first of its kind in Greece, and the founder of the school was called Sappho. She believed that women should be equal to men and that education was the beginning of equality. One day, while he was working in the school's olive garden, Sappho asked Katerina's father if he had any children. He told her about his only daughter and, at the same time, remembered the dream. He told the dream to Sappho, who asked to meet her. She did and afterward, asked him if she could educate her and make Katerina her scribe. It was customary for a scribe to write down the expressed thoughts of great men and women. Sappho, in addition to founding her school, was recognized as an accomplished poetess.

Katerina was a bright and energetic student and, as the years passed, she worked closely with Sappho and wrote down the important information the girls received, as well as the discourse of the day.

In the fullness of time, both Sappho and Katerina would be long forgotten. However, the Oracle's prediction would not and in 1970, a baby girl named Kathleen was born in Santa Fe, New Mexico. Her mission would unfold after she learned the life lessons that would provide her with the knowledge, skill, and empathy to heal and bring peace to a very troubled world by training a very select group of women to bring about needed changes.

As part of the preparation for the completion of her mission, Kathleen would spend one week with a man many believe to be a legend or a myth. This man is a Buddhist monk, a man whose life is dedicated to the service of others; a man whose unique ability to heal was recognized through the name given to him by the abbot of his monastery. A man he called "The Gifted One."

After her birth, Sappho and the Oracle smiled down from a world that exists far beyond us and, at the same time, within us. Their smiles were the result of the joy they felt knowing that Kathleen had arrived to complete a mission which had its roots long before the birth of Christ.

CHAPTER 1

Kathleen

From the time she was a little girl, Kathleen always thought that someday she would do something really important. It wasn't that she heard a voice or saw a vision. It was an awareness; something in the all-knowing recess of her heart that informed her. It was something that could not be turned off, nor ignored. Most of all, it was something that could not be changed, unless she refused her appointment with destiny.

She knew that someday, like Gibran's Almustafa in *The Prophet*, the ship's horn would sound and something extraordinary would be asked of her. Until that time, her life would be spent in preparation for this event. It was exhilarating and, at the same time, scary; it was something she had never shared with anyone. It was her secret.

The awareness had been there for as long as she could remember. Growing up, she also knew she was different. She saw and felt things that didn't matter to most kids, but they mattered to her. Cruelty, unkindness, lack of consideration for others, and hatred in all its forms were especially upsetting. She felt the psychological, emotional, and spiritual pain that those around her were experiencing. She was an empath, though she would have no idea what the term meant until her late twenties. As a child, she wondered why some people were nasty, or mean, and wanted to fix them. Like many people, when we're young, we think everything and everyone can be fixed. Only time teaches us to understand that some folks don't want to be fixed, changed, or healed. So it was with Kathleen.

Fiercely independent as a child, Kathleen set out on her journey, which was more like a mission. Her intention to understand and help others was linked to her feelings: sometimes feeling unquestioned love; sometimes rejection, and sometimes feeling misunderstood and alone.

Many of us work through similar issues. No one has the perfect parents, or family, and there's always a trade-off. In the homes of the settled and well behaved, life can be a consistent menu of meat and potatoes with little spice. In the homes of the free spirits, the daily menu is often more spice than sustenance. She had a portion of each and the ingredients produced a very unique personality: a young woman who in some ways thought like an old soul. The truth be known, Kathleen was, and is, an old soul, who chose to be born to her parents.

As a child, people were drawn to her beauty. Her mother used to say that she attracted boys like flies to sugar, and yet her relationships as a girl, and later as a young woman, usually didn't work out the way she wanted. She often wondered why all the learning and self-discovery hadn't provided the answers. Only later, in fact much later, did she understand that her relationships were designed to teach her about herself. She had no idea the schooling would take as long as it did!

Decades passed and she wondered if the thoughts she had as a little girl were just a childhood fantasy. It wasn't until she was almost forty-five that she felt the start of a process that would draw her like a magnet toward her "little girl" thoughts of being on Earth for a very important purpose.

This is what happened! She wanted to take a cruise to Europe, but it didn't seem possible until the last minute, when magically everything seemed to fall into place. While on the cruise, she dreamt of meeting a very special man who would teach her about life; teach her about the feelings she had as a little girl, and at the same time, answer her many unanswered questions.

Over a year had passed since the voyage. However, every few weeks, the dream would recur. She would awaken thinking that the dream is so real. There's something to this!

The early spring had been unseasonably warm and muggy. Kathleen needed to get to the local bakery to purchase a cake for her niece's birthday. The bakery would close in ten minutes and she was concerned that she wouldn't make it in time. She parked and, while running toward the bakery, saw an elderly man who was dressed in a raggedy, black raincoat. He was rummaging through a street-side, garbage receptacle. She had smelled the foul odor before she recognized its source when he turned to her and asked, "Madam, would you have any spare change? I seem to have left all my cash at home and it is my customary time for supper!"

She was about to respond when her eyes met his. His eyes had no pupils, only a deep, emerald-green iris, and as he spoke to her, she sensed that something was wrong. She had never seen eyes like his. It was as if he were from a different planet. The cake, the smell, the eyes, and the request for money…her mind was in overload and there was no time to sort it out. She also noticed that the foul scent had been replaced by a freshness that reminded her of a pine forest after a rain shower.

Being impolite wasn't part of Kathleen's social repertoire, but she had to get the cake before the bakery closed. She wanted to give the old man some money, but she also needed to get to the store before closing time. Before she could decide what to do, he said, "Here, take these with you; they will help you to see more clearly! Get your cake and I'll have what you really need when you return!"

Her mind was racing as she thought, *How does he know I'm getting a cake? There are lots of stores on this street.* Followed by: *There's no time! I've got to keep moving.*

The elderly man handed her a pair of glasses that looked like something Benjamin Franklin might have worn, except that they were tinted light blue. She held them in her hand and rushed to the store just as the baker was putting the key in the door. He waved, as if to say, "Sorry, we're closed!" She raised her hands in front of her, palms up, in the supplicant position, and pleaded through the glass door, "Please, I need a birthday cake! My niece's birthday; She's ten!"

There was a moment of suspense, as the baker debated his next action and then unlocked the door. His face looked like the before picture for an Ex-Lax commercial: tight, like a dried up prune. Then he said with what seemed to be a German or Swiss accent, "You are late. It is after six. I should not be doink dis. It vil give odders da wronk idea!"

She pointed to the cake she wanted. It already had "Happy Birthday" written on it in pink. *Close enough*, she thought, followed by *Writing Sandra's name on the cake is not going to happen.* The tension emanating from the Cake Nazi was palpable, and she would not ask for any additional consideration.

She played with the glasses as he began folding the cardboard into a box. She decided to put them on and look at herself in the mirror that faced the baker. She was stunned! Without thinking she said, "Wow!" in a voice loud enough for the baker to hear. He said, "Is der somethink wronk?"

She was able to see his thoughts! When she looked at him, she could see what he was thinking without trying. It wasn't like they were written or spoken. She just knew.

She said, "Your son is going to be okay! Don't worry!"

"Vat did you say," he said with a quizzical look.

"Your son, the Marine based in Afghanistan, he's going to be okay! You're worried about him!"

As soon as the words left her lips, she realized what had happened, but it was too late. The bird had flown from the cage and could not be returned. She was embarrassed and, at the same time, amazed at the power of the glasses.

She paid for the cake, picked up the box by the strings, thanked him for letting her in, and was headed for the door when the man came around the counter to intercept her. She moved quickly and made it to the door before he could get there. He called after her, as she was passing the garbage bin where she met the old man. He was gone! She had a five-dollar bill in her hand to give to him. However, she noticed a manila envelope sitting on top of the garbage. It had her name on it in what looked like an old English script—*Kathleen.*

She picked up the envelope and kept going. She thought, *What could I say to the baker? "These glasses allow me to read your thoughts!"* He'd call the psychic police and they'd banish me to Sedona, Arizona where I'd be sentenced to work for itinerant gypsies at Psychic Fairs for the rest of my life! Her mind worked like that; sometimes she would make things seem worse than they were.

Unlocking the car, Kathleen put the cake on the front seat and threw the envelope on the back seat. Off to the party, and the cake was enjoyed by all. It was only on her way home that she remembered the glasses she had placed in her purse, not to mention the envelope she had thrown on the backseat. She couldn't deny that there was something very special about the glasses, even though a part of her wanted to forget about the bakery encounter, she couldn't. She thought, *it's all just too weird.* She stopped at a traffic light and looked for the glasses. She couldn't find them! She turned the purse upside down on the front seat; still nothing. She wondered, *Why am I so upset?* There was certainly no denying it; she was very upset. It was similar to the feeling some of us have when we can't find the car keys after we've searched everywhere imaginable.

"Slow down Kathleen! Take a deep breath!" she said to herself and thought *They're here somewhere!* Just then, she looked down at the floor on the passenger's side and, sure enough, they had fallen out of her purse. She breathed a sigh of relief, not really knowing why. For reasons not fully thought through, the glasses had become very important to her. Maybe even a treasure?

Then she wondered about the envelope. She thought, *How did he know her name and how did he write it so elegantly on the envelope? How did he know she'd find the envelope? What was in it? It feels like a book. I'll open it when I get home.* Her mind raced as she tried to make sense of the pieces of the puzzle which, at the same time, remained a mystery.

She remembered the baker's face when she spoke about his son. She remembered feeling foolish for telling him what he was thinking. Her thoughts were flying like bullets on a battlefield. After arriving home, she went to the refrigerator for a glass of lemonade. Drink in hand, she sat at the kitchen table and opened the envelope.

She placed the glasses on the table next to what looked like a very old, or maybe, ancient book. It had a worn linen cover and smelled like the spice chest in her grandmother's house. The black print was handwritten perfectly. Someone had taken the time to print each letter as if it were part of a painting that would hang in a museum. It read:

> Thank You for Your Gift
>
> My name is Theophane and it has been my task to travel the world and find people who will be brought to the next level. To do so, they will be taught to overcome their life challenges and heal themselves in preparation for their work. You are being rewarded because it was your intention to give me a gift. It was not necessary for the gift to be received, but only that it was your intention to do so. My job is to travel the world and reward acts of kindness from people who expect nothing in return. In your case, the reward is very special indeed!
>
> You wondered about my eyes! Yes, I am blind, but in many ways I see more than most. My father and his father, and the fathers for centuries before him, were blind. We have been using this book and books like it for a very long time. The names of those who accepted the challenge are listed on the last three pages and signed in their own hand. We hope to add your name to the list.

She turned to the signature pages that looked much older than the text, read the names, and recognized that some of them were written in Greek or Latin, and for these an English translation was printed in black fountain pen next to each. *This can't be!*

> If you accept your training and pass, you will be asked to add your name to the list. Whether you accept or not, keep this book safe. If you choose not to embrace this challenge, a messenger will be sent to retrieve the book. If you accept your mission, you will give the book to your teacher. There have been many teachers. Your teacher's name is identified on the card placed inside the cover.
>
> There is a list of everyone who has passed the first test and been offered our gifts. Some accept the challenge; some refuse. Many of those who chose to move to the next level have

changed the course of human history. You have an opportunity to become one of them.

Currently, there is a man in training who, after the completion of his initiation, will sign a book exactly like this one. After your training, you will be asked to sign your book. There will be one last initiate, a young and very gifted African-American girl. After her work with us, she will also be asked to sign a book. Each of you will be involved in a process that will bring about much needed changes that will impact every man, woman, and child on our planet, as well as Mother Earth, herself.

You have many questions about me and I trust the following will answer most of them: As a young man, my father told me that our lineage goes back to the Golden Age of Greece. He said that our forefathers believed our blindness can be traced to the Legend of Tiresias. Supposedly, Zeus, the king of the gods, was arguing with his wife, Hera, about who enjoyed lovemaking more, the male or the female. Tiresias was known throughout all of Greece for his wisdom. He had also spent seven years as a woman. He was changed into a woman by Hera after she saw him hitting copulating snakes with a stick. No one was exactly sure why his action made Hera angry. Seven years later, he was later changed back to a man, after leaving the copulating snakes alone when he saw them. Since he had experienced being both a male and a female, he was consulted and asked to settle the dispute between Zeus and Hera. He responded, "Why the female, of course: nine times more than the male!"

Hera was angered again because Tiresias revealed woman's greatest secret when he said, "Of ten parts, a man enjoys one only." Hera thought his response was impious. It was not the response she wanted and in punishment, she struck Tiresias blind. Zeus, not being able to restore Tiresias' sight and feeling responsible for his wife's action, decided to give him the gifts of insight, prophecy, and understanding.

According to my father, his father told him that, since that time, every male in our family has been blind. The female children are sighted, and every generation has had a Theophane, the translation of which is "One Who Speaks with God." Every Theophane has used this book, or a book like it. Originally, it was printed in Greek.

As my male relatives before me, I am able to see clearly into the minds and hearts of those I have been assigned to meet. Because you have been given this book, you have passed our first test. However, there are more. For a variety of reasons, many do not complete the training. Your problems, suffering, and worries have provided the raw material for your transformation. However, your kindness, compassion, and instruction will create the alchemy necessary for your graduation to the next level.

Just as there have been many Theophanes, there have been many teachers. You are not obligated to contact the teacher identified on your card. In fact, do not make contact unless you sincerely desire to know the real reasons for your earthly concerns, as well as their solutions. The price you will pay for your knowledge will be that you must give up all your excuses and become who you really are without pretense. As a result of your training, should you make that choice, you will want to spend the rest of your life serving others and thereby, you will experience joy and satisfaction in living, as well as find all the answers you seek.

Do not contact your teacher unless you have decided to walk past your fear and step into the unknown. I promise that your journey will be fulfilling beyond your dreams. The choice is yours.

Blessings,
Theophane

Kathleen thought, *Magic glasses and now a book that looks like it belongs in a museum and will help me to change the world. All this because I volunteered to get my niece a birthday cake. Wow!*

She remembered seeing a card holder, similar to those used on the inside of a library book to hold the reader identification. She opened the holder and noticed that it contained what looked like a business card. She removed it. Written in gold leaf on linen-like paper in the center of the card was: "The Gifted One." The lower left corner listed a phone number and the lower right corner stated: "By Appointment Only." At the upper right- and left-hand corners were golden fleur-de-lis symbols. There was no address or zip code.

She thought, *I could use a little vodka in this lemonade* and, after taking her own advice, felt its warmth as it settled in her stomach.

Regaining her composure, her mind wandered back to the glasses that sat on the table next to her. She had a strange feeling, as if the glasses were watching her. She looked at them and felt energized, but at the same time very nervous. She sensed that her "little girl" dream was on its way to becoming a motion picture that had just begun—a movie that would take over her life and provide experiences and situations far beyond her imagination.

CHAPTER 2

The Decision

The "magic" glasses were a blessing and a curse! Kathleen wore them once when she went to a mall and it was overwhelming. The women thought about her weight, clothes and hair, while the men's thoughts related to her legs and breasts. In fact, there was an older man who looked like the TV character, Mr. Rogers, whose thoughts were so lascivious, that when she walked by she said, "You ought to be ashamed of yourself!"

He looked shocked and said, "Excuse me?"

She returned his question with a look that could douse a fire, and kept walking. Knowing what other people were thinking was exhausting; though she did appreciate the thoughts of a George Clooney type, whose immediate thought after seeing her was, *I wonder if she's married?*

She hadn't been at the mall more than ten minutes when she decided to put the glasses in her purse. She wanted to concentrate on her shopping and the glasses had her on overload.

A little over a week had passed since she met Theophane and she was mired deeply in the decision-making process. Given the chance to do something potentially life-changing was exciting, but at the same time, as scary as her first teenage date. She wanted to go and yet, she didn't; back and forth, over and over, the benefits and the potential problems. She thought, *Maybe this is all some kind of weird scam? Maybe I'll end up in some sultan's harem in a desert tent with other American women who had been similarly duped. Maybe I'll have to spend the rest of my life feeding the sultan grapes, washing his feet, and God knows what else? I need to get to a mall.*

The decision-making process had entered a stage of paralysis. Like putting her index fingers in a Chinese puzzle, the more she tried to run away from making a decision, the more she felt compelled to do so. And then the release!

She had made the mistake of wearing the canary-yellow high heels she always wore with her matching business suit when doing a presentation at work, and her feet were killing her. She had to sit down. It wasn't a question of whether she should sit down now, or a little later. She could feel that the big toe on her right foot had blistered and would need a Band-Aid just to make it home. She spotted an empty chair near the fountain that served as the focal point of the mall. She headed for it like a Jehovah's Witness spying a potential convert on their front porch, but an elderly man with a cane beat her to it. There were no empty chairs left!

When he hung his cane on the side of the chair, and turned, he realized that he had almost bumped into her. With recognition of the near collision, he said in what sounded like an unidentifiable European accent, "Forgive me madam, I've taken your seat! My apologies! I don't see that well."

He was tall, very tall and exquisitely dressed in a light grey suit with red-patterned tie and matching pocket handkerchief. His sunglasses seemed unusually dark, almost black, and his white shoulder-length hair was not typical for a man whose clothes seemed corporate.

He stood up without the aid of the cane and looking straight ahead he said, "You must take the seat. I insist."

"That's so kind of you, but I can't. I'm okay!" Followed by, "I'll find another one."

Just then, a teenage girl, who had purple hair, holes in her dungarees, a ring through her nose, and was sitting next to the elderly man, spotted her girlfriend, jumped out of the seat, and squealed, as only a teenage girl can, "Wendy, wait up. I've been trying to find you!" She was gone in a flash and vacated her seat. Kathleen sat and the discussion was over. As he took his seat, he said, "So Kathleen, you have been having some trouble deciding to take the invitation."

She responded, "What?"

"The invitation I gave you over a week ago to help us change the world."

She replied, "How do you know my name? Who are you?"

"I'm the raggedy man who asked you for some change that I might purchase something to eat for my supper. Remember you were on your way to the bakery? I gave you the glasses and the book."

She had forgotten the pain in her toe, but now it came screaming back as she tried to process everything going on.

Then, she remembered the glasses, his glasses. They were the same as the ones worn by the beggar. And the voice—it was the same, although his appearance was quite different.

He answered in a tone that was reassuring, "I am Theophane and you have read about me in the book I gave you. It is your karmic destiny to answer this call to service for which you have been preparing for many centuries."

Many centuries? she thought. *How could I be preparing for many centuries to do anything? This is crazy!*

Theophane continued, "You have come to us from another time and place. The story of your reincarnation had been foretold by the Oracle at Delphi over twenty-five hundred years ago. You were the scribe of Sappho, one of the first women to realize the power of the sacred feminine. During the Golden Age of Greece, when only men were educated, she founded the first, shall we say, Mystery School for young women. You spent your time with her and recorded everything she said and more. I say more because in the many conversations you had with Sappho, you also learned how she thought. She was quite exceptional, you know."

"So you're the man who left the envelope with the book?"

"I am!"

"Why are you dressed so differently?"

"Because you passed the test: You were kind to someone who appeared to be vulnerable and not able to do anything for you. And, it's fun to wear disguises. I have more than an adequate supply of them and they bring me great joy. They make me feel like I'm on stage. Like an actor."

"But I didn't give you any money! How did I pass the test?" she said.

"You didn't have to. I knew by your voice that you were going to do so after you finished at the bakery. It was your intention. It is always about the intention."

"How did you know I'd be at this mall at this time?!"

"I know many things, Kathleen, and my job, the reason I'm here, is to remind you of your job and the requisite preparation that going to the ranch will provide."

"This is too much! I'm a regular person."

"You know that is not true, Kathleen. Since you were a little girl, you have known that you have a very special purpose. You have had an awareness deep within you that a time would come when you would be called upon to do something that frightened you. Yet, it is something that must be done if you are to fulfill your destiny."

She couldn't deny it and thought, *He's right, but that doesn't make the decision any easier.*

And when the pounding in her toe began again, she turned away from Theophane to get a Band-Aid from her handbag that she had placed on the fountain wall. As she did so, she said, "I don't disagree with anything you've said and the feeling of doing something important has always been with me, but taking a week off to meet someone I don't know in the middle of the desert makes my stomach upset."

She took off her shoe and her stocking toe was torn above the offensive blister. She was able to get her toe through the opening and apply the Band-Aid. Mission accomplished, she turned to Theophane but his seat was empty. He had vanished. There was no sign of him!

Kathleen thought, *This is getting spookier by the minute. I wonder if I'm part of some metaphysical game show and, if I pass all the tests, will win a washing machine and dryer?*

The pounding in her toe had stopped with the removal of her shoe and she sat to contemplate her recent twilight zone experience. She was having difficulty making sense of it all and decided to do what any intelligent, mature woman would do in this situation...call her girlfriend. She had Nancy's number programmed in her cell phone and only had to dial "N." After the phone had rung five times, she thought, *Nancy, I really need to talk to you, so pick up the damn phone!*

As if she had rubbed the magic lamp and the genie responded to her wish, Nancy said,

"Hi Kay, what's doin' sweetie?"

Kathleen didn't know how to respond to "What's doin'?" *Where do I start?* she thought, *With the magic glasses and the baker? Maybe the letter I found on the garbage can? No! Though usually a tea drinker, this required a real drink. Some wine. Yes! Some wine would be good!*

And she said, "Nance, can you meet me at Hendrickson's?"

Real friends always know when something is not right and Nancy said, "Kay, are you in trouble? Your voice sounds strained."

"I don't know Nance! All I know is I need a Nance fix. I need to talk and I need to do it now. Help me!"

"Where are you? I'm at the mall sitting next to the fountain."

It was about six on Wednesday evening and Nancy was on her way to yoga class when the phone rang. The urgency made her feel like she was part of a SWAT team preparing to talk someone out of jumping off a bridge. Her home was only about a mile from the mall.

"I'll be right there sweetie. I'm just leaving the house!"

Kathleen hung up the phone and waited. It was good to sit and even better to think that her best pal was on the way. She felt numb. Hundreds of pansies, in a variety of colors, were planted next to the fountain and their perfume had worked its way to her olfactory lobe.

The fragrance was delicate and reminded her of her grandma, who loved her garden and for whom pansies were one of her favorites. Her grandmother had been very special to Kathleen because her mother never really had time for her. With one brother and two sisters, there was always someone interrupting, but with Grandma it was different. She had all the time in the world. She was born in Dublin, Ireland and still had, as she would say, "bit of the brogue!"

Grandma's house was an oasis because it was quiet and when

Kathleen went to visit she always welcomed her with the same greeting, "Kathleen, would ya like a cuppa tea, darlin'?"

Her house was meticulously clean and neat. Her grandmother took great pride in her home and used to say, "Ya know darlin', wit the Irish, dere's da shanty and da lace curtain. Wit me mom, it was cleanliness is next to Godliness!"

Kathleen was remembering the smell of Grandma's fresh baked bread when she saw Nancy entering the front door of the mall. She laughed at herself because she mused it was like a Lawrence of Arabia scene where the hero rides in on a horse swinging a sword. In her case, the heroine entered wearing Adidas and yoga pants.

Kathleen and Nancy went to Hendrickson's, a small German bar just outside the food court. They both ordered a white wine. Kathleen started her story after the first glass and it got easier to tell during the second. Nancy listened and nodded. *Nancy was always a good listener!* Kathleen thought.

When it was done, the great catharsis, Kathleen and Nancy were both a little looped.

It was time for Nancy to speak.

"Kay, this sounds like a movie script and what worries me is the ending. I've never thought of you as the reincarnation of anyone, never mind someone from Greece twenty-five hundred years ago. Look, I'm a waitress and I know something about people, but a blind beggar who morphs into a sophisticated businessman isn't something I see at the diner."

Nancy said, "Let's get something to eat at the food court before we drive home. It's cheaper. No use getting a DWI to top the day's events!" The next hour was post-climactic and Kathleen remained conflicted.

I need a sign! Something that tells me it's okay to go.

Her grandmother had been a huge proponent of the sign theory. That if you pay attention when considering a matter of importance and ask for divine guidance, something will happen. You'll be shown the way. But you have to be open to it and you have to pay attention.

Before she went to sleep that night, she asked the Creator for a sign. And as she drifted off to sleep, thoughts of her Grandmother's house, the smell of freshly baked bread and the white-haired lady with the smiling eyes, who had a story for every significant life challenge, brought her comfort.

Kathleen worked as a production manager for a reality TV series that focused on celebrities that had overcome addictions. The viewing audience was shown the star as he or she went about their day, either at home or on the set for a movie. She both liked it and hated it. It was fun! Except for having to cater to the spoiled whims of some of the celebs, it didn't seem like real work. Not all, but some were like overindulged brats, and to make things work she sometimes had to coddle them and let them think that their nonsense was really important. She had to be an actress.

When she arrived at work the next day there was a note on her phone: "See Ronnie ASAP!" Ronnie was her boss and could have easily won a neurotic contest. He always looked like he was on the verge of vomiting. He worried about everything and let most folks who came into his space know about it. Saying he was a little tense gives new meaning to understatement.

"Morning, Ron!" She said after a perfunctory knock on his open door.

"Come on in, Kathleen, we've got a really big problem!"

Kathleen was unfazed because everything with Ron was always a really big problem. She had no idea the problem would be her sign.

He opened the top drawer of his desk and took out a ChapStick that he applied to his lips—one of his many idiosyncrasies because he did it hundreds of times a day.

Compulsion satisfied, he repeated, "Kath, we've got some trouble. Really big trouble. I don't know where to go with this!"

The anxiety she recognized as her face flushed was the emotional Geiger counter telling her something was really wrong. This time it wasn't Ron having one of his mini breakdowns about something silly.

He unbuttoned his shirt collar and took a swig of Diet Coke from the omnipresent can on his desk. *Doesn't he know that stuff isn't good for him and he's always so worried about his health? He drinks enough of it every day to fill a kiddie pool!*

Ron cleared his throat and said, ""We're in big trouble! And I mean with a capital T."

Oh God! Please don't let him lapse into song.

Ron was a show tune fanatic and, when he considered it appropriate, would burst into song related to the occasion at hand. She held her breath and wished.

He didn't and continued, "T. Blake has fallen off the wagon after ten years of sobriety. His fans are devastated. T's been the poster boy for clean and sober living for so many of our viewers and now, he has to spend some mandatory time with Betty as a result of a DWI that almost killed an eighty-two-year old woman coming home from church.

Kathleen knew that Betty meant the Betty Ford Center. Ron always smiled impishly when he called the Center, Betty. He thought it made him sound witty, but for anyone who had to hear, he sounded like a jerk!

Before returning to the task at hand, he applied another coating of ChapStick to his lips.

"Kathleen, our parent company wants to sell us as a result of the scandal and, while I suspect we're going to be picked up by a New York station, everyone has to take two weeks off without pay. You need to tell your people. I'm sorry!"

The flush in her face had become a knot in her stomach with the realization that this was the sign. She had been with the station for almost five years and now, just when she needed it, at a time when it would usually be impossible to get away, she was given her ticket to ride.

Kathleen didn't respond immediately, and it made Ron even more nervous. He was afraid the potential job insecurity might move Kathleen to the camp of one of their competitors. He took a Kleenex from the box on his desk and dabbed his forehead.

"Ron, it's going to be okay! Everything happens for a reason and, as my Irish grandmother used to say, 'One door closes and another opens.'"

The admonition to go with the flow seemed to have no effect on Ron as he continued to dab and said, "I hope you don't decide to leave Kathleen, we need you around here."

A strange calmness had come over Kathleen. The flush in her face and the knot in her stomach were gone. There was something otherworldly about it, but she didn't know what. She had no idea that the recent life events were being manipulated by forces beyond her control and understanding. She knew she would be making the call to the number on the card and it now felt right. Only the fullness of time would tell her whether, or not, her intuition was on the mark.

When she left his office, she thought she got a whiff of Grandma's perfume and she smiled knowing for sure that when one door closes another opens. She hoped it opened to somewhere she wanted to go!

CHAPTER 3

Boston Lou

A week had passed since I returned home and, aside from reading my journal and thinking about what to do next, I went to work, told everyone the educational conference was very interesting, and successfully dodged any questions that would incriminate me and lead anyone to believe that I was somewhere other than where I had pretended to be.

Saturday morning arrived and the newspaper, *The Sand Paper*, announced that Tuckerton Seaport was sponsoring an event that afternoon called "Picken on the Porch." I had been there before and knew that for a five-dollar fee, I could listen to a group of musicians: young and old, beginners and professionals, play country and bluegrass selections on banjo, guitar, and fiddle. I had nothing on my schedule and decided to go, not having any idea of the bizarre surprise coming my way.

By the time I had arrived, they had already begun playing, and a white-haired man in his seventies was singing, "My Account's Been Settled Long Ago!" while also playing bass fiddle along with a group of fifteen musicians accompanying him. They followed his lead and his performance captivated the audience… No one spoke. When he finished, the applause was enthusiastic. In the three times I had attended this event, this was the first time I had heard a gospel song performed.

Observing the audience, I noticed that almost everyone wore dungarees, lots of plaid and work shoes or boots. Everyone except a short, stocky, middle-aged man whose complexion and features suggested he might be Italian or, maybe, Middle Eastern. He wore wire-rimmed glasses, Dockers slacks, a tan cap, expensive, cordovan leather penny loafers, and a starched blue shirt with the Polo Ralph Lauren logo.

I thought, *This guy doesn't fit!*

I was curious. I had never seen him before and, because I knew some of the regulars, I asked if they knew him. "Nope, never seen him before!" or a variation thereof, was the consistent response.

Hum!

My curiosity was heightened and I decided to take action. He was sitting alone and I had to pass him on the way to the coffeepot. A five-dollar fee entitled all attendees to all the coffee or tea and pie or cake they could eat. I asked him if he'd like a cup of coffee, since I was going to get one for myself.

He responded, "I'd appreciate that, Andy! Cream and two sugars would do nicely!"

I was startled, *How does he know my name?* but before I could ask him, he said, "Coach sent me!"

Evidently, he had been taught the same mind-reading skills demonstrated by Star and the Coach because he answered my question before I could ask it.

Without my saying anything, he responded, "It's easy when you raise your vibration!"

I needed some process time and decided to hold my question about raising one's vibration. I went to get the coffee as a young guitarist, no more than nine or ten years old, played a solo and soulfully sang the Freddie Fender classic: "Before the Last Teardrop Falls." He included the lyrics Freddie sang in Spanish and delivered it like he was born in Mexico. The kid was good! Really good! When he finished, even the other musicians applauded.

I returned with the coffee and sat on a rickety, folding wooden chair next to my new best friend. I took a sip of the coffee and asked, "How'd you find me?" As soon as I asked, I thought, *That was really stupid? You spent a week with the Coach and you have to ask about how he found you? The Coach knows where you live!*

But how did he know I'd be at the Picken on the Porch Concert? I didn't ask and instead said, "You obviously know something about me, but I don't know anything about you. I don't even know your name?

As soon as the words passed my lips, I thought about the Coach and the test he put me through by calling me Joe. I remembered how he told me he called all female initiates Lucy; however, he never spoke of a woman who had gone through the same initiation process as me.

I remembered how the Coach had said that our names don't capture our spirit energy and how, when he was ready, he would give me my Indian name.

He responded by saying, "The name that my parents gave me in this lifetime is Lou, actually it's Louis, but everyone calls me Lou. I received my Indian name from Coach; however, for now, Lou would be fine!"

His manner was polite, polished, deliberate and almost genteel; however, when he raised his cup and sipped his coffee, I noticed his right hand had multiple stitch scars and his knuckles were callused—two appeared to have been broken. His speech, manner and dress were incongruent with hands that appeared to belong to a street fighter.

Before I could express my observation, he said, "Before I met Coach, I was not a nice person!"

He spoke about his past and explained that he had been involved with some, what he called, "bad people" in Boston and, though his Italian complexion was like that of his father, his mother was Irish. He had attended Boston University where he earned an MBA and had received a full scholarship for weightlifting and wrestling. He explained, with a faraway look in his eyes, that in the seventies, he became a power lifter and trained in Russia with some of the greatest strongmen in the world.

His introduction was interrupted when the musicians returned. I wanted to hear more of his story, but for now, I sat back and decided to enjoy the show.

A tall, thin, sun-baked man in his fifties opened with the Willie Nelson song, "Tougher Than Leather." He sang it with a two-pack-a-day resonance in his voice that Willie would have liked and he articulated so clearly that, I believe, everyone in the room could hear every word. Lou and I listened as the story unfolded and presented its life lesson.

The song is about a gunfighter (Old Tougher Than Leather), who seems heartless and kills a young cowboy in a gunfight. The cowboy's girlfriend places a rose on his chest. Old Tougher Than Leather picks up the rose and crushes it. The young girl cries. But eventually, toward the end of the song, he dies one night from a poison inside, brought on by the wrongs he had done.

The crowd liked him and, if the applause had been registered on a meter, he would have been among the top performers of the day. Lou and I sat in silence, listening to the music, for about twenty minutes before he said in a soft and almost apologetic voice, "I'd like to talk to you outside!"

We sat on a homemade bench in front of the hall and he said, "You've learned that there are no coincidences!"

"Yeah," I responded. "That was one of the first topics Coach and I spoke about!"

He waited about three seconds before he said, "I was a lot like Old Tougher Than Leather before I met Coach. I did a lot of bad things and hurt a lot of people. I've been given a gift that I did not deserve because, unlike him, I didn't die from a poison inside. I was saved from myself by the hand of the Creator."

Who was this guy? It doesn't add up. What's he supposed to do for me and what qualifies him to continue the coaching that started in Arizona?

I hadn't finished my musing when he continued, "I'm going to answer all your questions, but for now, Coach wants you to know that he sent me because he knew you'd need some additional coaching. He wants me to remind you to read your journal daily. I was also asked to tell you that Star mentions you often and that you are not forgotten."

With that, he extended his hand, shook mine, said, "I'll be in touch!" and turned and walked away.

I was in shock. I had questions, but I knew they'd have to wait and I knew that it would not be in my best interest to try to do anything other than watch him slowly disappear into the trees that circled the parking lot.

My curiosity getting the best of me, I wanted to see where he went and, about two minutes after he left, I walked toward the trees. On the way, I saw a group of Girl Scout Brownies about age 7 or 8 with their mothers. They were looking at a bluebird on a low-hanging branch.

I walked past them toward the trees where I had seen him vanish. On the other side of the trees, there was no place for him to have parked a car and the trees bordered a river that could not be crossed without swimming.

Where he went and how he got there were questions with answers that were beyond me.

Another missing piece of the puzzle! I thought.

CHAPTER 4

Cupcake

On Monday, a week after I met Lou, I was sleeping soundly when I heard the phone ring. It was still dark and calls in the middle of the night scare the hell out of me. From the red digital display of the clock, I could see that it was 4:30. My heart was thumping as I said, "Hello!"

"Are you still sleeping?" The voice asked.

"Who's this?" I responded.

"Lou, your new best friend!"

"Is something wrong? It's 4:30 in the morning."

"Yeah, something's wrong. You're still in bed. Coach wants you up at 4:30."

I couldn't believe it! My new coach was giving me a wake-up call.

"Lou, you seem like a really nice guy, but you're starting to annoy me. If I want a wake-up call, I'll check into a hotel."

There was three to four seconds of silence, and I said, "Are you there? Did you hear me?"

"Look, City Bear, get your lazy ass out of bed. I'm sitting outside your house and at 5:00, I'm gonna ring your bell. I need to talk with you. There was something in his voice and choice of words 'ring your bell' that I found unnerving."

Lou's voice had an edge to it; he sounded like a collector for the mob and I hadn't made my weekly payment. I felt like I was on my way to an ass whooping. I put on the coffee, shaved, showered and dressed, all in record time. At 5:00, the doorbell rang.

"Good morning, sunshine!" he said with a grin that told me he enjoyed pushing my buttons.

He extended his hand to shake mine and the firmness of his grip suggested he could crush a cue ball if he wanted to. As he passed by me, I had the feeling I get when I'm standing next to the lion or tiger cage at the zoo. No question about it, though he was attempting to be cordial, this guy was dangerous.

"Would you like some coffee?" I asked.

"Certainly!" he responded.

We sat at the kitchen table. He took his coffee black; I had mine with cream.

"So, why am I here? That's what's going through your mind? Am I right?"

"It's a little unusual for someone to call me before dawn and tell me to get up because he's waiting outside my house."

Coach knows you have an affinity for the crib and he wants me to break you of the habit. He wants to make sure you get things done. Early morning is prime time and until you get with the program, I'm gonna visit you every day!"

Oh Geez, I thought. *A visit every day at 4:30 from the son of Godzilla is not my idea of a good time.*

"You can think of me as the son of Godzilla!"

Holy moly, like the Coach and Star, he can read my mind!

"I'm sorry about that!" I said.

"No problem! I've been called worse. You only thought it! Let's get down to business. You don't have forever, City Bear; none of us do. However, in your case, we need to get the ball rolling because if we don't, an awful lot of people are going to be in serious trouble."

I was about to say something that might have sounded whiney and decided against it. Instead, I said, "Lou, don't you think it would be nice if you told me who you are? How you know the Coach and what, exactly, you're supposed to do for me?"

"That's why I'm here, Cupcake. I mean, City Bear. Sorry about that! In my old life, I had the habit of calling civilians—people not in my business—Cupcake. I'd call them cupcake to insult them and see how they handle it. It's like an instant personality test. Like a verbal

Rorschach test. Some folks pretend they never hear it. Others are obviously angry, but don't say anything, and some come back at me and tell me off. It's interesting! It's a habit of mine that pops up now and then. Okay! I'm gonna answer your questions, but first let's see what kind of coffee you make."

When he took a sip, I noticed that on his right pinky finger he had a gold nugget ring whose top formed a horseshoe that served as the setting for a large diamond. He wasn't wearing the ring when I met him at the concert in Tuckerton. I would have remembered it.

While I was making a mental note of the ring, he continued, "Your coffee tastes like something died in the pot. But it ain't bad! Maybe whatever it was gives it a little extra something. Anyways, about five years ago, some of my colleagues and I were involved in a work project that didn't turn out the way we had planned. As a result, the FBI questioned us, and because one of these partners thought that I was going to be a snitch, he tried to have me killed. For the record, I never would have been a rat. Anyways, the attempt didn't work and I almost bought the gentleman who attempted to do the deed a one-way ticket to the happy hunting ground, if you get my meaning."

I thought, *This guy is a study in contradiction. He knows that the Rorschach is a test to identify psychological issues and yet, prefaces sentences with the word "anyways."*

It was past five in the morning and I thought, *This is surreal. I'm talking with a gangster from Boston, who is hiding from the mob in the Pine Barrens, who was sent by the Coach in Arizona.*

"Yeah, I understand!" I answered, while holding my coffee cup with both hands, so he wouldn't see them shaking. I was attempting to act insouciantly, as if our meeting and discussion were no big deal. I didn't want him to know I was scared silly and then remembered, he reads minds!

With my thought, he said, "City Bear, you gotta relax. I'm here to help you. That was the old me. I'm not that way anymore. If I wanted to hurt you, it would have been done already. My cousin, Anthony, remember Anthony the Monk who makes the sauce? You read the story he wrote. He's my cousin from Brooklyn; his mother is my father's sister. When he heard what happened to me, he set me up with Coach. I spent two years with him in Thailand. That's where I met Coach! Nobody thinks of looking for a guy like me in a monastery."

I felt like I was watching a movie from above and I was one of the characters. As his story unfolded, it became more like a movie script. There were definite similarities with his cousin and I would have loved to be a fly on the wall for family Christmas or Thanksgiving dinners. I could envision the patriarch putting a revolver on the table and saying, "If any of youz start to argue, or raise your voice, I'm gonna shoot ya. Now, let's have a nice meal but first, little Maria is goin' to say grace!"

After his admonition to calm down, he continued, "Anyways, I meet with Coach, who loves Anthony, and he talks to me about my life. He asks me if I have much money and I say, 'Yeah!' He asks me if I have a lot of powerful friends and again, 'Yeah!' He asks if I have made love to lots of beautiful women, and again, 'Yeah!' Then he says, 'Money, power and women and you are not happy!' It was like a kick in the stomach; he was right. I was miserable, but there was also something about the way he said it that made me recognize the truth. I realized I was always searching and never found what I was looking for because I didn't know what it was. You can't find something if you don't know what you're lookin' for."

I couldn't make this up. It's too far out! This is Rod Sterling stuff!

Lou liked to talk and I listened. Before I got involved with the wrong people, I was a world champion powerlifter. In the 1980s, I spent time in Russia and trained with some of the strongest men in the world. For me, the strength came naturally. I was born with it and at the age of twenty-five, I felt very comfortable with my Russian friends; however, my mother got sick, she had no hospitalization, and my cousin Vinnie, offered me a no-show job with a trucking company, where I got benefits that included myself and my mother in a family plan. I collected money and never did any trucking work. A few times, when there was a really big score and they needed an extra man, I was invited to participate."

This was getting better and better. My hands had stopped shaking, as I listened to his story. I was wondering what happened with the Coach in Thailand, when he said, "I'm getting to that. Be patient!"

"Anyways, I always loved opera and, as a kid, my mother made me play the accordion. I was pretty good at it, but I really loved opera. I know this is goin' to make you laugh, but sometimes when there's a really beautiful aria, my eyes get moist. I'm helpless, like a baby. Can you believe it? Me…with moist eyes?"

Moist eyes. This is really something. I thought. *He can't say "cry!"*

He continued, "I met Coach and he's everything Anthony said, and more. The guy is unreal and I wanted to hang out with him forever. It was like meeting God—only better, because I wasn't dead.

"Before I forget, what Coach wants you to do is to write seven stories that will provide women, who will be attending a conference in Greece, with the inspiration to think of ways to change the world. That's your mission. The stories shouldn't be real, but rather stories about what could be if women thought outside the box. Stories that will motivate women to recognize they have the ability to bring about needed changes within themselves, their families, community, workplace, and the world.

"When I return tomorrow, I want to hear about what you did today that is in keepin' with what Coach taught you. I'm also gonna tell you about a guy I met in the joint who changed my life.

"That's enough for today, Cupcake. I mean City Bear."

He smiled at me and nodded as he walked toward the door.

This guy is like a character from a movie and I get a kick out of him. I was looking forward to hearing about the guy who changed his life like a kid sitting around a campfire ready to hear a ghost story.

CHAPTER 5

Namaste

She couldn't sleep! Her mind was racing out of control like a runaway freight train downhill: the scene at the mall, her meeting with Nancy, the note from Ron, the T. Blake scandal, and the smell of Grandma's bread—over and over. There was no stopping it. She felt as if her mind did not belong to her and had become under the control of the sorcerer's apprentice.

She knew she was going to make the call. It was a done deal. But the morning seemed light-years away. She decided that sleep was not in the cards. According to the clock, it was only 2:17 in the morning. She decided to go to the kitchen for some tea and the leftover piece of pastry she had brought home from the mall. On the way, she picked up Theophane's book from the chair where she had left it.

The smell of the hot tea helped and, after a small bite of the pastry, she held the book with both hands and felt its weight and texture. It was heavier than it looked which she attributed to the covers that were much thicker than ordinary book covers. When she opened it, she noticed the metallic fleur-de-lis emblem on the back inside cover. She hadn't noticed it before.

She read the entire book again and focused on the three empty spaces for additional signatures on the back page. She scanned the names already listed above them and stopped when she read the English translation for a signature written in what appeared to be French. It was Joan of Arc. *Is this possible?* And with a closer look the reality of what she had in her hands became evident: Archimedes, Lao-Tzu, Socrates, Mary Magdalene, Charlemagne, Michelangelo, Abraham Lincoln, and of more recent vintage, Chief Joseph, Mother Teresa, and Nelson Mandela. She finished the pastry, put down the book and held the hot tea in both hands. *Wow!* She thought, *What the hell am I getting myself into?*

She went back to bed, but it was useless. She tossed, turned and watched the movie in her mind that replayed without request. When she couldn't take it anymore, she got up, showered, dressed and went back for another cup of tea.

She had checked the area code for the number on the card in the book and it was for an Arizona listing. She waited until 10 a.m. and made the call.

"Hello Kathleen!" the woman's voice answered. "We're delighted you will be coming to visit. As you know by now, you have some very important work to do." The voice was perky and welcoming. *The voice of someone I'd like to spend time with*, she thought.

"Do you have a pen and paper?" she asked.

"Yes, I do!" Kathleen answered.

"Good!" She was given the date and the directions to the ranch and the instruction that she must arrive at 4:30 a.m. on that Sunday morning. A few minutes before would be acceptable; however, if she arrived after that time, she would forfeit her opportunity to work with the Gifted One and another candidate would be contacted.

She could feel her heart pounding and her hands getting sweaty. *This is a little intense! Jesus! In one breath I'm welcomed and the next told to get out of town if I don't make it on time. Maybe I should say no thanks now and save myself the trouble of having to work with time Nazis!* Her mind flashed back to memories of the Seinfeld's Soup Nazi and she smiled.

The voice continued, "Don't let the time thing throw you; there's a reason. You'll understand when you get here. And, by the way, my name is Star and I'm really looking forward to meeting you."

Kathleen was preparing to respond when she heard the click. Star had hung up!

She told her friends and family that she was going to Arizona to visit a girlfriend from college. It was plausible and everyone knew about the job layoff. Of course, Nancy knew the truth. Someone had to know and initiate the search-and-rescue operation in case she didn't return. Nancy knew as much as she did and, while sworn to secrecy, she also had the phone number and directions.

Kathleen decided to bring the magic glasses but not to wear them at the airport. Her experience at the mall taught her it could easily be overwhelming. She'd use them only if she needed to. It made her feel like some kind of superwoman. She laughed at herself as she mused about changing into a costume in a telephone booth for the purpose of foiling the plans of evil-doers.

The plane landed and it was early afternoon. She had plenty of time and, after she picked up her Ford F-150 at Budget, decided to go shopping. She loved to shop, especially for shoes. She was embarrassed about how many pairs of shoes she had—even Nancy didn't know.

She always wanted to have a truck but felt it wasn't practical. This was her opportunity. *If this experience really turns bad,* she thought, *at least I will have crossed off one of my bucket list dreams... driving a Ford F-150. Maybe in another life, I worked on a farm?*

The Oracle and Sappho had been following her progress and again, they smiled, realizing that she had been a farmer's daughter, but it was over 2,500 years ago when there were no Fords around!

Kathleen figured out how long it should take and traced the route on a map she had received from the rental company. There were no houses near the area identified as his home and it appeared as if he lived in the middle of cactus and rattle-snake country. She wondered where he got his water from. It appeared to be so barren!

It was time to leave and she took a deep breath as she started the engine. Soon it was pitch-black and the lights of the city faded. It was scary and, at the same time, exhilarating. *Let the festivities begin!* she thought, as she turned the F-150 onto a dirt road about thirty miles down the highway.

About a hundred yards in, a coyote startled her as it ran across the road. She knew the Native-American superstition that, if a coyote runs in front of you, it's bad luck. After the fright, she said out loud, "Oh crap!" and thought, *Is this a bad omen that I should pay attention to?*

She had kept the windows closed and the air conditioning on

because she was terrified of bugs. If a bug had flown into the truck, she would have wigged out and needed a Xanax to recover.

As the miles clicked by, the directions were right on: Make a left here; a right there until she sees the ranch—but she didn't. Her heart began to race. She figured there wasn't another soul within fifty miles and if she couldn't find the house, not only would she be driving all night, she would miss her date with possibly the most interesting man in the world and have to go home.

When she went to check the map, she noticed the glow of a light above the berm to her right. The berm was about ten feet higher than the road and, after she got out of the truck, she climbed up and saw the ranch and the porch light that had served as a beacon. With the glow and the simplicity of the ranch, she was reminded of a scene from a Thomas Kinkade painting. *It doesn't feel scary,* she thought. *Maybe the coyote was really a dog. Do dogs count?*

She was forty-five minutes early and decided to lock the doors and close her eyes. The flight had tired her out more than she knew and within minutes she fell asleep—a deep sleep. The minutes ticked by and the magic hour was approaching fast. In her dream state she heard someone call her name. Startled, she awoke wondering if it was real. There was a moment of figuring out where she was followed by an adrenaline rush that preceded her looking at her watch. It was okay! It was 4:25 a.m. She left the truck and walked toward the door. She was ready to knock when she saw the gunmetal fleur-de-lis door knocker at chest height—the same design that was on on the back cover of the book.

She lifted the knocker and knocked. There was no sound. The sun was about an hour from rising and it was the darkest hour that comes just before dawn. She waited. No sound.

She decided to knock again and, with the first knock, she heard steps on a wooden floor that creaked. She expected a man. When the door opened, a woman in a white cotton dress with green beaded trim and matching moccasins offered her hand and said, "Hi Kathleen! I'm Star. You are on time. Come in! He will be right with you!"

Kathleen thought, *She doesn't look like a maniac, maybe this won't be so bad?*

As Star left, Kathleen could hear footsteps coming her way as she waited in the hallway. Standing there, she smelled the scent of sandal wood and heard the faint strum of a guitar and Willie Nelson singing "Seven Spanish Angels."

The footsteps stopped and he appeared at the end of the hallway. He was about five-nine, five-ten and rugged, looking like an outdoorsman. He had a crew cut and sunglasses with a denim shirt that had raggedy sleeves cut down to just above his elbows. The silver cowboy belt buckle had what appeared to be a bear claw design with a representation of the globe in its palm. It was surrounded by seven stars in the shape of a horseshoe. *What's that buckle all about?* She thought.

"Welcome Kathleen!" And he extended his hand.

Then it hit her. *What do I call him? Do I say, 'Thanks, Gifted One?' It sounds weird, almost dorky!*

Before she could answer, he said, "By the way, please call me Coach. Everyone calls me Coach. Those who gave me the name were well-meaning, not realizing that in America the name sounds like I should be a porn star. Something they had never contemplated."

As they shook hands, Kathleen said, "Thanks for inviting me, Coach. I hope I can learn whatever it is you have in mind." She wondered whether it sounded flirty, which she didn't intend it to—at least she didn't think she did.

She wondered how Coach had seemed to recognize that she didn't know what to call him. *An unanswered question! Perhaps, mind reading?*

Willie's voice got louder, as she followed Coach toward the rear of the house. She said, "That's one of my favorite songs! I'm a Willie fan!"

Coach responded, "Where I grew up they love everything cowboy. Willie has been around a long time and I was a fan before he became the outlaw and wore a suit and tie. We are going to get along, Kathleen, and I promise that when you leave at the end of the week, you will not be the same person you are right now!" He gestured toward the door of her room and said, "You will find everything you need and your bathroom is down the hall to the right. Get settled and rest. In about forty minutes, you will hear bells. After the bells, you have ten minutes to come to the room at the far left end of the ranch. We can then talk more!"

He gave a slight bow with his head and said, "Namaste!"

She answered, "Namaste!" and thought, *What an interesting man. Namaste. "The Buddha in me recognizes the Buddha in you!" Hum! He's very good looking. I wonder if Star is his girlfriend, or wife. Maybe I'll want to stay another week!* She had to put her thoughts in check before they took her to places for which she was not ready.

While she was unpacking and putting her clothes in the pine chest of drawers that looked like it was from the forties she wondered what he had meant when he said, "you will not be the person you are now."

She draped her blouse and jeans over the chair next to her bed and pulled off her cowgirl boots. Shopping for the boots had been fun. They were her first pair.

She put on a thin white cotton robe that had been laid out on her bed and decided to lie down and get some rest. The movie projector in her mind had shut down and she felt surprisingly relaxed.

The faint tinkling of the bells awoke her before she heard the knock at the door. She sat up, straightened the robe and said, "Come in!"

Star was holding a tray that had a cup of steaming tea, a small, silver milk server and sugar, as well as three miniature temple bells that hung on a metal stand, and a tiny wooden drumstick. She smiled and without saying a word, placed the tray on the night table next to her bed. She moved swiftly and silently. Kathleen found it interesting that she didn't say "good morning," or "hello," or something.

She put some milk and sugar in the tea and took a sip. It was very hot so she decided to go the bathroom to freshen up before the meeting and let the tea cool.

When she arrived at the meeting, he was already seated to the right of the fire that was providing heat for the room. He gestured for her to sit on the rug next to him and about five feet from the fire.

"Close your eyes, Kathleen."

His voice was soothing and calm; the voice of a radio announcer who had it all under control. She noticed he had changed his shirt and wore a white, long-sleeve dress shirt with a button-down collar and the sleeves rolled up. He smelled like Bay Rum, the old-fashioned aftershave barbers splashed on their customers after the haircut.

After what seemed like maybe three or four minutes, he said, "Do you smell the fire?"

"Of course!"

"What does it smell like?"

"A wood-burning fire. I like the smell!"

"And Kathleen, have you thought about where the smell comes from?

"Not really. It comes from the wood. It comes from the burning of the wood."

She was getting a little annoyed and thought, *Maybe I won't want that extra week if this is going to be a non-stop, metaphysical show-and-tell seminar. I'm not sure this is what I signed up for.*

As the thought passed, he said, "Kathleen, I know this might seem trivial, but bear with me. My questions are directed toward a purpose and if you will suspend your judgment of me, I believe you will be more than satisfied with the end result."

She recognized a sense of uneasiness. And she thought, *He seems to be able to read my mind. This is the second or third time it's happened. Maybe it's just a coincidence.*

Then he said, "Kathleen, the smell of the fire is the smell of the spirit of the wood as it returns to all that is and all that ever will be. It's the smell that took as many years as the tree is old to develop. It is the unique perfume of the tree that is created by the seasons, the sun, the rain, and the storms. It is the tree offering itself in death to the Creator and with its fragrance saying, "This is what I have experienced. Thank you for my life and thank you for the opportunity to warm this home and the people in it as I return to You."

My God! she thought, *that was absolutely beautiful and poetic. My thoughts of burning wood in a fireplace will never be the same.*

She was still enjoying the recognition of her new awareness

when she heard him say, "Open your eyes. Look at the fire and tell me what you see?"

She was more tolerant this go-round and answered, "A beautiful fire! The flames seem to have a mind of their own and it seems that no two are alike."

"So you see the light of the fire?"

"Yes! It's quite beautiful!"

"Do you see the darkness that surrounds it?"

"I really wasn't paying attention to the darkness, the flames were so pretty."

"Now look at the darkness."

"Yes, I can see it but it takes more effort."

"Kathleen, without the darkness, the flames would not be able to show their beauty. It is in the contrast that they show themselves and delight us."

Where is he going with this? she thought.

And in the next second, he responded, "We need the sunshine and the darkness; the agony and the ecstasy. We need our problems and challenges, so that we can provide solutions. The light and the dark are family and each has a role to play in our lives. Sometimes we curse the darkness not realizing that without it we would never be able to fully enjoy the light. We are thankful for the light; however, as we understand more fully, we become equally as thankful for the darkness."

Wow! This is good stuff. It's like good therapy. When you leave the therapist's office and all the way home, and maybe for the next day or two, feel high about understanding something that was right in front of you that you never saw; something that was obvious.

She was swimming in her thoughts when she heard him say, "Today, breakfast will be at nine. Get some sleep. Usually, breakfast is at eight but today, you need a little more rest." When she returned to her room, the clock read 6:03 a.m. As she slipped beneath the yellow cotton sheets, she wondered how she could ever explain this experience to her family and friends.

CHAPTER 6

Alone

It was a week later and early in the morning. I was already dressed and brushing my teeth when my phone rang.

"Cupcake, are you up?"

"Yeah, Lou! I've been with the program since your visit."

"Very good! I'll ring your bell at five. I've got more to tell you." And he hung up.

I laughed at myself for thinking about the first time I heard him say, "I'll ring your bell!"

Promptly at 5:00 a.m., the bell rang. I poured a coffee for him and one for me. We sat at my kitchen table. Lou said, "I want you to know my story. I'm a really good example of how people can change while we're still in the 'getting-to-know-you' phase of our friendship."

I didn't know we were going to be BFFs, I thought, *but I could live with it! I enjoyed his company, even if he was a little scary.*

"I want to tell you about my first coach, Pops," he continued, "whom I met before our coach. When I first met Pops, he was sitting alone in the prison library. When I walked by him, I said, 'Hi!' But he never looked up or acknowledged me. He just kept reading, but I couldn't see the name of the book.

"About a week later, I saw him again. This time he was sitting at a table in the dayroom. He was alone and reading again. When I walked by him on the way to the laundry, I said, 'Hi Pops!' Again, there was no response. Pops acted as if he were deaf, or conditioned not to answer. I had learned his name from one of the young guards who liked to talk non-stop. His nickname was Squeaky because he had a high pitched, annoying voice. He told me that Pops had killed three men who had robbed and murdered his wife. He and his wife owned a grocery store and the thieves came in just before closing. The cops said they had no leads and, after some months, as there was still no resolution, Pops decided to do his own detective work. He hunted them, like the animals they were, and every time he killed one, he put a brown grocery bag over the guy's head. After the third guy was bagged, he called the cops and waited to be arrested.

"Now, I knew I'd be inside for about three years, give or take time off or on depending on my behavior record, but that was before Cue Ball decided to terminate my stay. Here's what happened: As I told you before, I had taken the job with my cousin to get medical benefits for my mother. I had been a world class powerlifter and was invited by the Russian Government to work out with a group of men including Vasily Alekseyev, considered by many, at the time, to be the strongest man in the world. I loved it there and the guys were terrific. I was thinking of applying for Russian citizenship when the call came. My cousin, Vinnie, told me that Mom was in bad shape and needed an operation. She had no medical coverage. My dad had died when I was in my teens. Mike's trucking company would put me on their books and I wouldn't have to actually work; just show up once in a while and help out with a job. Of course, the job would also involve doing something that could get me sent to the slammer.

"It so happened that we had a plan to relieve a local drug dealer of some of his merchandise and found ourselves in the middle of a Federal sting. I was offered a reduced sentence, if I ratted. I didn't take it and was about three months into doing my time when my colleagues decided they couldn't trust me; that I knew too much. I'm not a rat and never would have been, but they had other ideas and sent a lifer, whom everyone called Cue Ball, to do the deed.

"I was in the shower and always kept my back to the wall and my eyes open. I could see Cue Ball walking toward me and trying to hide something in his right hand. I could smell it. I knew it was coming, so I made like I'm closing my eyes and washing my face. I timed it and waited until he was about two steps away. Then I turned to the side, opened my eyes and saw that he'd already got the shiv in place. As he went to stab me, I circled into him and with both hands grabbed his arm. I got his wrist, twisted and broke it, took the knife and stabbed him in the ass. I'm not a killer. The Russian boys had taught me well. They loved martial arts and, when we weren't training with weights, we trained in the arts.

"So, there's Cue Ball, with his shaved head, lying on the wet floor screaming with a broken wrist and a shiv in the cheek of his rear. While I'm finishing my shower, the guards come running in and yelling. There's blood all over the place and the youngest of the guards shouted, "Who did this?" Of course, no one answers and everyone in the shower is questioned about what happened. Nobody saw anything! No surprise!

"When it was my turn to be questioned, I was really pissed. I was doing my time, had never ratted and yet, somebody didn't trust me. Okay, I thought. I'm gettin' out of here early because I'm tellin' everything I know and screw them for what they tried to do to me.

"After the questioning in the principal's office—I always referred to the warden as the principal—I phoned my lawyer and put the wheels in motion for payback. These things don't happen overnight and I knew it would probably take a few weeks…at best.

"Now back to Pops. So, for the next week, I saw Pops here and there and, unless he's working in the kitchen, he's reading and was always by himself. I noticed he read with a pen, which he uses to underline or mark things. By now, I've said hello eight or ten times and he never looks up.

"I figured he's about sixty, five feet ten, and one ninety. He's a clean shaven, light-skinned black man with a crew cut. He's at his usual spot in the dayroom and as I walked past I said, 'Hi Pops!' He looked up and said, 'That's the ninth time you've said hello, even though I didn't answer! Sit down. I heard about your friend's accident in the shower. I always thought the guy was a pain in the ass and now, he's got one!' He laughed and shook his head.

"For the first time, he looked up from his book and into my eyes. He smiled and said, '*Inhumanitas omni aetate molesta est!*' followed by, 'Inhumanity is harmful in every age! Cicero. The bastard had it coming, Lou. Nice work!' My mind was spinning. *A convict who quotes*

Cicero in Latin? Who is this guy? That day, Pops became my new best friend and after the shower incident, no one bothered me. I know Pops had something to do with my being left alone, though he never mentioned it.

"Before my early release two months later, I came to know Pops as the most interesting person I'd ever met and I miss him. I was his student and he had a great deal to teach; however, as I heard him say many times, 'You can't teach anyone anything, unless they want to learn. You, and they, will know when they're ready. Some are never ready!'

"In the months that followed, I learned more about life and people from Pops than I had learned in all my MBA classes at Boston University—my family could never have afforded the tuition. I told you I was a wrestler and powerlifter. I had a full ride for tuition and books, as well as a part-time job in the library.

"Pops and I met every day from two to three. After lunch and before dinner, he had an hour off. We always sat at the same dayroom table and no one ever tried to sit there. It was always available and no one ever came by to talk to us.

"Early on, I told Pops about Boston University, and he replied, 'Your nickname is Boston Lou!' I liked that! Boston Lou! When he smiled, his gold, left, front tooth was visible and I remember thinking that you don't see many people with gold teeth anymore!

I asked him why he was always reading. Before answering, he said that he had been inside for five years and had fifteen to go. He had never been interested in books until he got a job in the library. He picked up a book by Louis L'Amoure, an author famous for his stories about the Old West. After the first book, Pops was hooked. He knew L'Amoure's life story and admired him. He remembered reading about a time in the author's life when, as a young man, he had a job as a guard at a mine with lots of time by himself and used it to read.

"Pops told me L'Amoure interested him because he was a Renaissance man. Louis had been a prize fighter, merchant seaman, cowboy, guard, and many other things. He was also an amateur archeologist, historian, sociologist and geologist. Like Louis, Pops became interested in a wide variety of topics, including the classics. He had even taught himself to read the *Iliad* in Latin.

"I recall that during one of our sessions, he said, 'Reading has taught me that writers are immortal. As long as their words are written somewhere, and read by someone, they're alive. I decided that my time inside would be spent with the greatest minds who've ever lived and not with people who have no interest in improving themselves. I also decided that I'd rather be alone with my teachers in the books than anything else. You are the first person in five years I've had conversations with that are more than one or two words.' I was stunned. *The first person in five years. Wow!*

"Pops waited a few seconds and seemed to be lost in another world before he added, '*Otium sine litteris mors est et hominis vivi sepultura*. Leisure without literature is death and burial for a living man. That is one of my favorite quotes from Seneca. See what I mean? Seneca is alive today because his words live on through me.'

"'Didn't other inmates bother you?' I asked.

"'Oh, yeah! There was a young Spanish guy who used to taunt me. He'd come to my table in the dayroom and keep asking me questions. I never looked up or answered. It went on for about a week and everyone thought it was quite amusing. Then, one day, when he went to sit down, I got up quickly and got behind him and placed my arm around his neck and put a sleeper hold on him. I was so angry, I kept it on a little too long and the guards had to resuscitate him. He looked dead. They took him away on a stretcher. After that, no one ever sat at this table and no one attempts to engage me in conversation. By the way, I was an Army Ranger in 'Nam.'

"As we came to the end of the day's meeting, Pops said, '*Saepe creat molles aspera spina rosas*. This is a wonderful quote by Ovid that means *Often, the prickly thorn produces tender roses*. I hope our time together is productive!'

"He stood up and, carrying a copy of *Plutarch's Lives*, walked toward the kitchen. I was honored that he not only spoke to me but allowed me to sit on a plastic chair at his table in the dayroom.

"In the weeks that passed, I learned that Pops wanted to teach folks what he knew. However, there seemed to be few takers. I was the first and I looked forward to our daily meetings and discussions.

"During one of the meetings he told me he never felt alone because he spoke to his deceased wife every day. When he arose he would say, 'Good morning Sugar!' And at night, he would blow her a kiss and say, 'Good night Sugar. I love you!' During the day, when something interesting happened or if he read something that moved him, he shared it with her. He told me her real name wasn't Sugar, it was Dorothy.

"Pops never complained. Every day, he'd have a different story about a character in a book or someone in his life who had taught him something. Everything was always about learning. He was especially disgruntled with the major religions of the world and, although he knew I was Catholic, he liked to quote Mark Twain who said, 'If Christ were alive today, the last thing he'd be is a Christian!'

"I understood what he meant and shared his concern. Christ taught humility, helping the poor, forgiveness, kindness, compassion, equality, and tolerance. It seemed to me that not only the Catholic Church but many Christian churches, as well as other religions, have difficulty with tolerance and helping the poor. However, I also know that there are far more good people than bad, but every religion has its share of followers who treat others with contempt or unkindness.

"One day, I asked Pops why he spoke to his wife everyday? 'You know, Lou,' he said, 'We don't die; only our body dies. It's not just my wife I talk to. I talk to and pray for my friends and relatives who have passed. I know they're always with me and I'm looking forward to seeing them again. You know, we're never alone; they're always with us even though we can't see them and they really like it when we talk to them and remember them. When you love someone and they pass, you're never alone.'

"I had met with the Feds and their lawyers and had told them what they needed to know. It didn't make me happy doing it, but I felt I had no choice. I knew that what I told them would put some of my own family away, but if they tried to get me once, they'd try it again.

"Pops told me that if they offered me the witness protection program, not to take it. Instead, I should find a way to fly under the radar and disappear for a few years. He didn't trust the Feds and felt I'd be better off on my own. I agreed with him!

"The day before I was scheduled to be released, I had my last visit with Pops. I had the feeling he wanted to say something special to me that day and he did.

"He said, 'Lou, when you were involved with the boys, you had lots of money, didn't you?'

"I answered, 'Yeah! I had money to burn.' Then he asked, 'You had lots of power?' Yeah! 'And lots of women?' Yeah!"

Where was he going with this?

"Then he asked, 'Money, power, women—and you weren't happy, were you?'

"I thought for a minute and answered, 'No. I never felt good about myself!' Later Coach would ask the same question.

"'Well, then,' he said, 'maybe you've learned something! You see, Lou, if you don't love someone, you're not really alive. I'm alive in here every day because I will always love Dorothy. Lou, it is love that makes us happy.'

"He had become more than a friend. He was my mentor and brother. I could feel my eyes starting to get moist as the time for me to leave came closer. Suddenly, without warning, he stood up and extended his hand. He shook mine and hugged me. He whispered in my ear, '*Ut sementem feceris ita metes*, As you sow, so will you reap. Cicero.'

"The last thing I remember was him walking away to the kitchen carrying his copy of *Plutarch's Lives.*"

CHAPTER 7

Boot Camp

As requested, Kathleen was ready by 8:00 a.m. and was sitting alone at the breakfast table when Star came in carrying a wicker breakfast tray. It was beautifully arranged with a silver teapot, two porcelain cups, strawberries and blueberries arranged in a rainbow pattern, two bowls of oatmeal with cinnamon sprinkled on top, flower-embroidered linen napkins, and utensils.

"It's beautiful, Star!" said Kathleen as Coach entered the room and took the seat directly across from her. Noticing that there were only two seats, Kathleen asked, "Will you be joining us, Star?"

Star responded, "I will join you at lunch. I have to go to town early!"

Coach wore the same clothes he wore when they met and he seemed delighted that Kathleen had accepted the challenge. He told her about the problem he was having with the deed for the ranch and the motivation behind his trouble which was the ancient water well on the property.

She asked about the activities for the week and he told her that his training would be very different from that completed by the man who came before her. The guest he came to call City Bear. He also had to tend to some business and told Kathleen to make herself at home; he would return for lunch.

After breakfast, Kathleen took the opportunity to wander around the ranch and get to know the land surrounding it. During her exploration she thought, *I haven't seen one bug. That makes me happy. If there were lots of bugs here, I don't know what I'd do!*

The ranch was picturesque and when she came to the field of

wildflowers, she was awestruck. She wondered how he'd managed to create such a beautiful place. She knew it would be her first question upon his return. She walked for about an hour and took in the sights, smells, and sounds of the desert. *There's something very primitive here,* she thought. *It's real. No concrete, asphalt, noise, smog, smelly air, horns, sirens, stop lights, cell towers or people. Just Mother Earth in all her glory! I love it!*

It started to heat up and she decided to go inside and lie down. She was still tired from the trip. The chiming bells woke her at 11:45 a.m. and lunch would be ready at noon. She went to the restroom, brushed her hair, washed up and reapplied her makeup. When she got to the kitchen, Coach was already seated and Star was with him. There were three seats at the table and the menu included soup, sandwiches, and iced tea.

Coach told her that they would start the training after lunch and that she should bring a canteen of water, which Star would provide, and wear hiking boots, a wide brim hat, shorts, a long-sleeve white shirt and suntan lotion for her face, legs and hands. They met at the rear of the house at 1:00 p.m.

From where they met, the wildflower field was visible and Kathleen asked, "How'd you do this?" There isn't enough water here to support your beautiful garden!"

Coach explained the underground well that served as the centerpiece for his home, which had been a sacred place of initiation for the Navajo that had fallen into disrepair. He told her that some folks in town had found out about the well and, even though the land had been bought according to local property laws, they were trying to take it from him. He also told her that the people who wanted the land had lots of money and political power. After doing so, he sighed. A breath that seemed to say, "I'm releasing the tension I feel through my breath."

Kathleen could feel his anxiety and asked if anything could be done to protect his land. Coach answered, "I have gone to visit with some local medicine men and they are now working with me. We are doing prayers and songs to bring about the necessary protection."

Kathleen thought, *Prayers and songs. Where I come from you get the meanest and smartest lawyer money can buy and go for the jugular.*

Coach replied, "There are things in this world far more powerful than any lawyer, and the folks who are trying to take my ranch are in for a surprise."

More mind reading, thought Kathleen.

As they walked, Kathleen noticed that Coach seemed to move so smoothly it reminded her of watching a tiger or a leopard. His movement was fluid, easy, and yet powerful. She found herself being more than a little attracted to him, and when she recognized the feeling she reminded herself that that was not why she was here. It would not be the last time she had to set mental boundaries for her feelings about Coach during the week.

Coach told Kathleen that the first four days of the week would be spent learning survival skills. When she asked why, he told her that the beginning of the week would prepare her for the three days she would spend alone in the high desert mountains completing her vision quest.

She responded, "Alone! High desert mountains! Three days! Vision quest! What are you talking about? I'm a city girl. I'll die! I can see the headlines and the TV showing the rangers carrying my dead body, half eaten by wolves or bears, or whatever you have up here that eats people. And my mom and dad will be crying! No, I don't think so."

Coach let her rant and when she was finished he said, "You forgot the scorpions and rattlesnakes. They can kill you!"

With that comment, Kathleen responded, "Mother of God. Sweet Jesus! I think it's time for me to pack my bags and return to a place where I only have to worry about muggers and rapists!"

"Are you finished?" he said.

"I don't know. I'm still hyperventilating!" she responded.

"Kathleen, do you think I would let anything happen to you?"

"How can you protect me when I'm alone in the mountains, or in the valley of death, or whatever you call it?" she asked.

He invited her to sit in the shade of the only tall bush in the area. She scoured the area for bugs before she sat down.

Noticing his smile, she said, "This isn't funny! I should have been told that I would have to spend three days alone on some mountain. By the way, do I have food and water with me?"

He answered, "No, no food or water. That is what I am going to be teaching you about: how to find food and water."

"You're kidding, right?"

"No, I am not kidding. The challenge is for you to learn who you really are with no pretending. The vision quest will do that for you."

"You mean if I make it out alive?"

"Kathleen, you can go home now, if you wish. However, ever since you were a little girl you knew you were put on Earth to do something special. This is it and, if necessary, you must be willing to give up your life to complete your mission. Your true identity and the exact purpose of your mission will be shown to you during your vision quest."

It was weird, very weird, but a strange sense of calm came over her. It was a feeling of peace that she had never experienced before. She felt at one with everything and, when a spider appeared from a jumble of grass and cactus, she was unafraid. Coach put his hand in front of the spider and it walked over it, pausing only to drink some sweat. She was totally calm as she watched the spider go on its way.

Something is happening and I have no clue but I like it. I like the feeling of oneness with everything, she thought.

On their way back to the ranch, neither spoke, nor was Coach at the table for dinner, only Star. Kathleen had heard his truck leave about an hour before. At dinner, she talked with Star and they shared information about their lives and relationships. They continued to talk during their evening walk as they enjoyed the coolness of the sand under foot, the light desert breeze and the sky with more stars than Kathleen had ever seen. When they returned, Coach's truck was still nowhere to be seen.

Kathleen had brought with her a book that told the story of Quanah Parker and the rise and fall of the Comanche, the most powerful Native-American tribe in American history. It would serve as her companion during much of her free time.

Coach was back for breakfast and Star joined them. He was in a really jovial mood and later she asked Star about it. Star told her that the men who were trying to take away Coach's ranch and property had decided to walk away. Apparently, each of the three men had encountered something that frightened them. One man had an owl land on his kitchen window sill and peer in at him and his family during their dinner. When he went outside to chase it away, it was gone. Another man had problems with his electricity. Nothing in the house worked and, no matter what they did, they couldn't fix it. The third man looked out his bedroom window when he heard drumming and chanting late at night. He saw what appeared to be five Native Americans dancing, drumming and singing around a fire in front of his barn. When he went outside, there was no sign of a fire or people.

Kathleen thought about Coach's words: "There are things in this world far more powerful than lawyers."

During the next three days, Coach taught Kathleen how to find water in the desert, start a fire with sticks, a magnifying glass, a water bottle, a flint, and a flashlight battery. It was impressive! He taught her three ways to trap small animals and how to skin and cook them. He explained which native plants were edible and how to prepare a place to sleep to avoid scorpions, snakes and other creepy crawlers.

If anyone told her she would be capable of learning and doing any of these skills, she would have bet a week's salary against herself.

On the morning of the fourth day—the first day of her vision quest—she had made all the recommended preparations as she waited for Coach in the front seat of his truck. *There's something really primitive about him,* she thought. *I wonder if he'd like to spend the first night with me. He'd never go back to being a monk!* Kathleen smiled as the thought played out and she said to herself, "Bad girl Kathleen." Bad girl or not, the thought was fun, maybe even more than fun!

It took about an hour to get there and the terrain had changed. Still, the vegetation was sparse, but now there were mountains and valleys and in some places greenery. She could feel her heart pulsing in her neck and, even though the air conditioning was on, she could feel herself sweating. The truck stopped without warning and Coach said, "This is it!"

Kathleen thought, *This is it? Sweet Jesus,*—her favorite expletive—*there's nothing around for fifty miles. I'm gonna die!*

Without missing a beat, Coach said, "You are not going to die! You are going to learn who you really are with no pretense. You are taking the next step that will prepare you to do the job your destiny is calling you to. I promise, Kathleen, in three days you will not only be alive, you will be more alive than you have ever been in your life! I will be back to get you on Sunday at 6:00 a.m. Meet me here!"

It was now only about 8:00 a.m. and the sun had not reached its full potential. She had already learned a great deal from Coach and immediately began looking for greenery that might indicate that water was nearby. She looked down and into a valley about a mile away and saw trees with leaves and shrubs in a small, isolated patch. She took her gear and headed for it. Sure enough, there was a small pool seemingly fed by an underground spring behind some trees. For the next two days, she camped near the water and ate what vegetation she could find that she knew about. It wasn't much, and by the second evening she had placed traps for small game—rabbits or squirrels—around her camp. On the morning of the third day, she checked the traps which were still empty. By afternoon, she was hungry, dizzy and started to vomit. She wondered if the water, which looked clear and fresh, was actually contaminated, and as the chills started thought, *I'm going to be really sick and I'm alone.*

Coach was scheduled to come the next morning and Kathleen decided to retreat to a small cave overhang which she had spotted earlier. She decided to build a fire and make a wall of stones to reflect the heat against the overhang to get warm.

By the time she collected the wood and got the fire going, she was totally exhausted and sick. The vomiting continued and, when there seemed to be nothing left in her stomach, she passed out. She awoke when she heard the drumming. At first, she thought she was dreaming. Then, shadows of dancers appeared on the cave wall to her right, even though no dancers could be seen. Then, there was a voice.

At first, it was more of a whisper! As she focused, it became audible and it was a woman's voice. She said, "You are Katerina, the scribe of Sappho. Your last incarnation over 2,500 years ago prepared you for your mission. Your meeting with Coach is your final preparation. As the voice spoke, the drumming became louder and the dancing shadows more frenetic. Kathleen thought, *Is this a dream? Am I hallucinating?*

The voice continued. "You are wondering who I am. I was known as the Oracle at Delphi. I have watched you over the centuries and waited for this time. You will be protected and guided. You have nothing to fear. You are in the process of fulfilling your destiny. The glasses you were given will help you with your work in Athens. There, you will be teaching a very select group of women what they need to know to make long overdue changes in the world. So that you will know this is not a dream or hallucination, I have left you a sign."

Kathleen drifted off and when she awoke she found an eagle's feather stuck next to a Greek-looking building, or temple, that had been drawn in the sand. She remembered the voice mentioning a sign and she now knew deep within her heart that there would be no turning back.

She started to pack up her gear and Coach appeared in front of the cave.

"Are you okay?" he asked.

"Better than I've ever been!" responded Kathleen.

On the way back to the ranch, Kathleen asked, "Why is there a fleur-de-lis on the card, book and door knocker?"

He responded, "Our abbot knows that the world can only be saved by women working together, and one of the greatest woman of all time, aside from the mother of Christ, was Joan of Arc. Her spirit is with the women of the world as we prepare to make the changes. Like you, Joan did not choose her destiny!"

When Kathleen returned to the ranch, she met Star in the kitchen who looked really upset.

"Is there something wrong?"

Tears welled up in Star's eyes and she said, "It's my ex-husband. He pleaded with me to give him another chance and swears that he now goes to AA meetings every day. He always had a drinking problem but the first time he hit me was the day that I left him. He told me if I don't take him back, he's going to kill himself. He's crazy enough to do it!"

"What are you going to do?"

"I told him I would give him a trial period and see how it goes."

"Okay, so what's the problem?"

"I'm in love with the initiate who came before you, Coach calls him City Bear. I called him and told him that I'm giving my ex-husband another chance, and now I feel my heart is broken. I suspect he is in great pain!"

"How did he take the news?"

"He told me that my happiness is what's important and that I should do what my heart tells me. That comment made me love him even more. I've been sick to my stomach since the phone call. I want to do the right thing, but the idea of my ex-husband killing himself is more than I can handle."

"Star, I suspect your ex-husband will go back to his old ways and when he does, feel no remorse and leave him for good!"

Before Kathleen left, Coach told her that she would be receiving directions for her mission and he wished her good luck. She was about to go to the door when he said, "Those thoughts you have had about me, I have had the same thoughts about you…maybe, another place and time!"

She could feel her pulse quicken as she smiled at Coach and walked toward the door on her way to the truck and then drove on to the airport.

CHAPTER 8

Sailors' Delight

It was like some kind of sickness, but I couldn't stop thinking about Star. Maybe it was the love disease…and I wanted to go back to being normal when I didn't have to think about her constantly; however, no cure seemed in sight. I decided to keep busy…that would do it. If I kept busy, I wouldn't think about her and if I kept busy long enough, maybe the thoughts would stop? For a week after I met Lou, I wrote, exercised, cleaned the garage, cleaned the yard, marked papers for my university classes (I taught classes related to autism), and spent any down time reading. Nothing worked! Whatever I did and wherever I was, she was in my thoughts.

Okay! Keeping busy didn't work. So, what's next? Maybe I could trick myself into thinking that I was no longer interested in her? Maybe that would provide some relief? I would repeat a mantra extolling the value of no commitment and personal freedom. I decided on… "I am alone and free." Whenever my mind wandered to Star, I repeated mentally, "I am alone and free, I am alone and free."

I tried the alone and free thing for a couple of hours but my subconscious intruded and substituted "miserable" for "free." Every time I contemplated "alone and free," it came out as "alone and miserable." Strike two! I felt hopeless. I had become like Sisyphus rolling the rock up the hill, only to have it roll back down before reaching the top. My mind had become like a jukebox that played only one song. I wanted to pull the plug for some relief, but in the twilight zone of my mind, no matter how hard I tried, the plug wouldn't budge.

I played back conversations that Star and I had shared. I remembered the way she walked when she served breakfast or lunch, along with her scent, and it was making me wacky!

Maybe there's a pill I can take? I thought. *Someone at Hallmark Greeting Cards would know. Maybe there's a doctor for people who had become Hallmark junkies and had spent their entire paychecks on cards. They probably had meetings where I could go and share my feelings before going to work. I had to wait for Walmart to open before I could get a card. I'd tell them that I would stand outside the store shaking until I had the right card, and that I was hopeless, had hit bottom, and needed to change but didn't know how. Maybe I'd make new friends?*

It went on and on until I decided to do the unthinkable: I found Coach's number on the card given to me by Theophane and called her.

After a few rings and no answer, my heart sank and I started to feel sick. Then suddenly, she answered and I heard her say, "Hi City Bear, I was hoping you would call!"

The clouds parted and the sun smiled at me. I had been released from the prison of my mind—the sound of her voice was the key for the lock. I could feel my heart racing and my throat getting dry as I attempted to act carefree and casual.

"Hi Star! I miss you!" I said.

"City Bear, I am embarrassed to say it, but you are in my thoughts day and night," she responded.

I was so excited. I've never fainted, but everything was going black. *How absolutely ridiculous it would be,* I thought, *if I had to cut her off in order to dial 911 before I lost consciousness.*

I regained my composure and asked about Coach and the new initiate. She said that she liked having another woman around and that the next initiate was from Santa Fe, was fun to be with, very pretty, and highly insightful. Her past included working as a production manager for a TV reality series, as well as hosting TV and radio programs.

Wow! I thought, *TV and radio... the lady sounded interesting and since Star liked her, maybe we'd get along.* I had more questions about the new initiate but I didn't want to sound overly curious and decided to put them off for another time.

We spoke about Coach and his problem with the deed, her

father, the ranch and missing each other. The conversation was the pill I needed. I realized what I felt for her and she felt for me, and that was all I needed to go about my day with some degree of normalcy. We decided I'd call once or twice a week and the phone call gave me focus, direction and the energy to work toward my mission and help Coach.

The night I met Lou, I decided to weigh myself and take my blood pressure. Now it was time to do something about it. I had six months before my return to the ranch and become the person I always wanted to be with no pretending. Coach had become my mental, physical and spiritual advisor who had given me the ball and expected me to score with it. I didn't want to let him down and, even though my daily progress journal was heading me in the right direction, I knew I was now inspired—after my talk with Star—to do even better.

I was about to begin my plan for the day. In the morning, I read what I wanted to accomplish the following day and before retiring, I recorded my progress. Before forgetting, I also decided to record my memory of Coach—what comes to mind about who he is rather than his words—capturing the essence of his personality!

In a stream of consciousness style, I began to write as the following thoughts became clear: everything in his house was neat and organized; he began his day at 4:30 a.m. and usually, went to bed around 8:30 p.m.; he ate a hearty breakfast that included variations of eggs, turkey sausage, oatmeal, whole grain toast, low-fat cottage cheese and tomatoes. He usually ate a half sandwich of chicken, turkey, fish or roast beef and a cup of soup for lunch, and a dinner of meat and vegetables with fruit for dessert about an hour after the meal. I noticed he usually had a piece of dark chocolate for an afternoon snack and, if I was with him, he always offered me a piece. He chewed it, like everything he ate, slowly. While hiking and exercising, he always looked like he was having a great time. Sometimes, he'd play the air guitar and sing Willie Nelson songs in between exercise sets.

Having made a start on this description of Coach, I decided to continue cleaning and organizing the closets, the garage, my desk, my work area, and every drawer in the house. Coach had explained to me about the practice of *feng shui* which I wanted for my home. I knew it would take days, maybe a week to get it in order. It was now the beginning of the third week since I arrived home.

Today was also the day to begin my exercise and nutrition program, immediately after putting a small dent in what was called: Operation Martha Stewart, where I vacuumed, arranged, sorted and discarded until I could almost hear Martha say, "It's a good thing!" I wanted to build my exercise program based on what Coach had taught me. From past experience, I knew that any weight training had to be done in the morning; I didn't have the energy in the afternoon, and because of my schedule, getting up at 4:30 a.m. on Monday and Tuesday mornings would be difficult! Therefore, on Wednesday, Friday, and Sunday, I would alternate a push-pull weightlifting routine in the mornings and walk or ride the bike for an hour in the late afternoon or early evening on Thursday and Saturday. The push-pull routine would include kettlebells. On Sundays and Fridays, I would bike, walk or swim for at least one hour. I decided that every day, regardless of when I got up, I would begin the day with fifteen minutes of yoga and fifteen minutes of meditation. I knew the six months would fly by but, if I wanted to realize my goals, I had to start as soon as possible.

During one of our desert walks, Coach had mentioned that Star also meditated, was very regular with her yoga routine, jogged, and lifted weights three times a week. He told me that her first husband was a physical trainer at Gold's Gym in Phoenix and now it made sense: her lifestyle had contributed to her looking and moving as if she were twenty years younger than her age.

Since it was too late for a morning workout, I decided to go to the gym after lunch realizing that it would not be as good then as in the early morning, but I wanted to get started. The exercise left me feeling both invigorated and relaxed. I had the natural high that accompanies an intense workout.

Late in the afternoon, I decided to relax and sit on the dock overlooking the lagoon at the back of my house. The sun was setting and the sky was majestic with shades of red suggesting the next day would be a "sailor's delight!"

It was quiet—really quiet—and I thought how lucky I was to be relaxing, looking at the water, smelling the salt air and having time to reflect about everything that had happened before, during, and after my time with Coach. The silence was interrupted by the clear, crisp sounds of a trumpet echoing from the other side of the lagoon. The other side of the bay was about two miles away; however, sound travels long distances over water and I suspected the musician was celebrating the sunset and paying tribute to the disappearing orb.

I wondered whether the musician was a man or a woman, old or young, how long had he or she been playing, and what had prompted him or her to play for everyone on the bay and no one in particular?

I enjoyed the selections: the theme from *The Godfather* followed by an oldie, "I'm Gonna Sit Right Down And Write Myself A Letter," and one that was especially appropriate, "Summer Wind." I had heard Frank sing "Summer Wind" in Atlantic City and wondered if Ol' Blue Eyes was still performing in the hereafter and that maybe, just maybe, the folks who had led really good lives would get front row seats and those of us whose lives were a little shaky would have to listen in the parking lot.

Then, as magically as it had begun, the music stopped. Wanting to investigate, I jumped into my kayak and paddled to the far shore. As it got darker, I could see house lights go on in the distance. When I got closer, I could see that the docks were deserted. Whoever it was and from wherever the music originated, would not be discovered tonight. I paddled home and arrived in time for the mosquitoes that had announced not only that dinner was being served, but that I was the main course. I was annoyed at myself for forgetting to bring repellent!

The message was clear. Music would become part of my day or evening. I thought, *Music is a gift from God! It can have many purposes. Tonight it served to remind me of memories long forgotten but cherished. The music took me to a place that provided a sense of inner peace.* I wished Star had been there with me. It was later that night when Star called with the bad news about her husband.

CHAPTER 9

Theophane's Travels

Theophane had been traveling around the world like Santa Claus on amphetamines: Rome, Paris, Athens, Calcutta, Beijing, Kenya, Tokyo, Montreal, Bogota, and the list went on. Kolkata change his disguise as he saw fit, but the test was always the same: would the woman, his target, commit an act of kindness for someone who could do nothing for her in return? If she passed the test, she was given a book, similar to the one given to City Bear, except that it came with the names and contact data of the seventy women already chosen listed in the back. Sisters in spirit who would pick up the torch lit by a woman long ago at a time when Socrates walked the streets of Athens in search of knowledge, wisdom and truth.

Later, the book would serve as a directory for the women so that they could contact each other, if necessary, at otherwise unpublished numbers, emails, and addresses. The book was theirs to keep!

The introduction in each book was the same. It told the story of Theophane—his mission and lineage back to the legend of Tiresias. However, unlike the book given to City Bear, these books contained a section that was more specific concerning intentions and methodology.

It explained that seventy women would be chosen to attend a week-long meeting in Athens, Greece at the Hotel Grande Bretagne. The purpose of the meeting would be twofold: first, as a gift for their time, they would be instructed by a number of the world's leading health and beauty experts regarding methods for turning back the clock and appearing fifteen years younger; the second purpose was to receive an unusual training which would include topics, methods and procedures not discussed since the time of Sappho, the Greek poetess and facilitator of the first finishing school for women—a time in Greece when only men were educated. She is considered by many to be the first champion of the woman's rights movement and more than twenty centuries later, her teachings will be presented by a woman who spent her life as her scribe—a woman trained since childhood in the esoteric teachings and ways of her famed teacher.

The cover of the book each woman received appeared to have been made of linen and seemed old, from a much earlier time. It depicted an ink drawing of a classically beautiful, Greek woman holding an ancient key which pointed toward a keyhole situated in the middle of a representation of the Earth. Under the picture were five words: "Time to Challenge the System!" that were written in a stylized Greek manuscript.

Theophane loved to ham it up! Sure, he was blind and old; however, that didn't keep him from being a jokester. Sometimes he'd appear as a man, and at other times, as a woman. For disguises, he'd wear wigs and pretend to be a forgetful elderly man or woman. He'd wear a fancy suit and tie and pretend to be an eccentric salesman. He especially enjoyed the role of a missionary in Middle Eastern countries. Theophane loved life, and in spite of the importance of his mission, he had an attitude which suggested he did not take himself too seriously.

Furthermore, Theophane didn't have to select his targets, for he was presented with a list of names and contact information which were determined by a council of Buddhist monks, assigned by the abbot who charged Coach with his mission: to identify women around the world who had demonstrated a desire to bring about the needed changes. These brother monks were asked to review worldwide television, read global and national newspapers and scour the internet for women who demonstrated courage, intelligence and, most of all, a burning desire to create a better world for their family, friends and the world.

Not everyone passed Theophane's tests. There were many who appeared to be kind, compassionate, and willing to take on the job and many, when confronted with a request from someone appearing to be in need, who showed their true nature. One was a very high-level American politician, who treated Theophane with disdain, arrogance, and discourtesy, as if he were bug that should be brushed away and forgotten. After interacting with her, he told me that being married to a toothless, but kind, harlot would be preferable to waking up next to her!

Obviously, she made quite an impression and it wasn't good!

Since the island of Lesbos was the home of Sappho, you may be wondering why the gathering would take place at the Hotel Grande Bretagne. Lesbos was certainly considered, but there were no accommodations in all of Greece that could match the Hotel Grande Bretagne for elegance, history, and most of all, security. At a time in world politics where the threat of terrorism is omnipresent, the Bretagne has a history of hosting notables that demanded high security: members of the Kennedy dynasty, the poet Odysseas Elytis, Lyndon B. Johnson, Umberto Eco, Indira Gandhi, Francis Ford Coppola, Gary Cooper, Elizabeth Taylor and her husband, Michael Todd, Sting, as well as Sir Laurence Olivier, Aristotle Onassis, Prince Rainier and Princess Grace, and the list goes on!

The book also provided instructions related to program dates and times, as well as a request to contact the hotel by a given date to confirm their attendance. Each participant was also asked to sign a contract indicating their commitment to participate in the weeklong activities without absence or abbreviation.

CHAPTER 10

Coach's Letter

Dear City Bear,

The week after your visit, Star and I began training a woman whom Theophane met at a mall in New Mexico. My abbot has informed me that she is a very special woman and her involvement with us is critical. However, she has the freedom of choice and nothing in this life is guaranteed. Theophane met her at the airport in Seattle and, like you, she passed the first test; she was kind to someone who, at the time, she thought could do nothing for her in return. She was presented with the same book you received and in which you signed your name. Her name appears after yours with one remaining space for our third trainee.

Although Star and I knew she would be able to train with us immediately after you left, the successful completion of her training was not certain. If she did not complete the training, we would have had to work with another candidate. While Star and I have developed the ability to read thoughts, we do not have the ability to interfere with free will.

We are very pleased to tell you that her training with us has been successful and she has agreed to play her role in bringing about the needed changes we have discussed. She will be contacting you within the next few days to work with you toward the completion of your missions.

In preparation for her contact, know that the woman you will be working with is very unusual. She is the reincarnation of the scribe of Sappho; a famous Greek poetess who started the first "Mystery School" for women over 2,500 years ago on the Greek island of Lesbos. At the time, only men were afforded the opportunity of a formal education.

She has agreed to assist in bringing about the needed changes by working with a wide variety of women throughout the world. Some of these women have husbands who are very powerful in government, business, and banking, as well as a variety of important vocations. Many of these women have particular talents or abilities that have not surfaced. However, after their training, the world will hear from them. Some of the women have been chosen to be ground-breakers for our movement in opening minds and hearts toward re-evaluating policies and practices concerning the environment, health, peace, education, business, and religion. Others will work quietly, and by their example, provide beacons of sanity and compassion for our out-of-control world.

Theophane has made the requisite contacts and arrangements with the women. You will be invited to the week-long retreat in Athens where your stories will serve as part of the curriculum for their initiation into a new way of thinking about themselves and the world. Remember to visualize daily the completion of your mission.

With honor and respect,
Coach

CHAPTER 11

Hotel Grande Bretagne

The day had come when the women would meet each other in the Grand Ballroom of the Hotel Grande Bretagne. It was there that they would be introduced to a woman who is the reincarnation of Sappho's scribe and whose last incarnation was in the late seventh century B.C.E.

The attendees came from all walks of life and political persuasions. The rich and famous were represented, as were the less fortunate. Although over thirty countries were represented, the majority of the women were, what might be considered, mainstream American, and all of them spoke English.

It was exactly 8:00 p.m. when the lights dimmed. There was no warning, no announcement. When the room was completely dark, a spotlight appeared and in the light was a woman, about five feet, six inches tall with flowing blond hair to her shoulders and wearing a simple white tunic. Her glasses were unusual. They were octagonal and blue. They looked like glasses someone might have worn when the framers of the U.S. Constitution were busy at work. There was silence; absolutely no sound from the audience.

At first, the woman surveyed the room moving her head from side to side. She appeared to take a deep breath and said, "Welcome ladies, my name is Kathleen, though my name doesn't really matter. You're here because you've passed a test that made you eligible to attend. You're here because you all committed a random act of kindness for someone who appeared to be unable to do anything for you in return. You're here to change yourself and, in doing so, change the world! Welcome my sisters!" The women applauded.

In the minute or two it took Kathleen to introduce herself to the group, she had captured them! Whether it was her tone of voice or her manner of speech, they were "all in" though they had no idea, at that time, what she meant about changing the world.

Kathleen continued, "During the next week, you will learn more about yourself than you have in your entire life. You will learn about your truths, as well as your lies. Yes, we all lie—sometimes for very good reasons. The problem is not in the act of lying; it's when we believe our lies and attempt to fool ourselves that we, and the world, suffer.

"So, as promised, this week you will receive the finest treatment known to humanity to help you improve your appearance and health. You will also be given the tools you need to assist in healing yourself, as well our planet, bring about peace to all nations, and improve the lives of all with whom you come in contact. It's no mistake that you are here because what needs to be done can't be accomplished without you! Do not be afraid or doubt yourself! You will be given all that you need!

"After dinner this evening, you will be given a schedule of the week's activities. I have arranged to meet with each of you individually for one hour during your stay. The time and day of your meeting are listed on your schedule. You will also be provided with a dining room seating chart for you will be sitting with different people at each meal. After breakfast, you will be required to meet with a group of seven women until 10:30 a.m. The group will be different each day, and you will be expected to introduce yourself to the other women in the group, provide them with your contact information, and share with them what you would like to see changed in our world. Lunch will be served at noon.

"At the time you are scheduled to meet with me, you will excuse yourself from your group and return when we are finished. Because of time constraints, meetings had to be scheduled morning, afternoon, and evening

"During the afternoon, appointments have been made for you to meet with a variety of specialists in the following areas: nutrition, meditation, exercise, intimacy and sexuality, problem solving, world affairs, communication, and planning. I promise that, by the end of the week, you will think and act in a manner about which you may have only dreamed. You will have the knowledge, skill, and ability to do what the world needs in your own unique way. You will be ready to complete your mission!

"Dinner will be served at six each evening, and immediately thereafter, I will speak to all of you as a group. The information I present will be the distilled wisdom of my time spent as the Scribe of Sappho. While hard to believe, I was the Scribe for this famous woman over twenty-five centuries ago and have reincarnated to work with you to make needed world changes.

"After my talk each night, you will be given a copy of a story that will help you begin the process of thinking outside the box. It will be a story of a woman, who made a difference. I ask that you read this story just before you go to sleep because I want it to be the last thought on your mind before you drift into the arms of Morpheus."

There was some movement and shifting in the room that suggested Kathleen's announcement had made some women uncomfortable.

"Dinner will now be served!"

That was it; short and sweet. The spotlight dimmed, the room darkened, and when the lights went on, she was gone.

The following morning, in her meetings with individual initiates, she wore the blue glasses. They had become an important tool that allowed her to see beyond the illusions that each woman had created in her life. When she spoke to them, she often felt as if someone much older and wiser was speaking through her. Her remarks were always on target because, as the reincarnation of Sappho's scribe, she had at her disposal the wisdom of the great poetess, as well as the thoughts and realizations of the young woman chosen to memorialize her words into written form. And, of course, the glasses gifted to her provided laser-like insight.

During the week after their sessions with Kathleen, the women talked to each other about their experiences. No one was disappointed and they marveled about her ability to strip them of their distortions about themselves and others. They were intrigued that she told them about personal faults, or inconsistencies, in a manner that could not be refuted or denied. It was as if they were emotionally and psychically naked before her. It was like trying to lie to God. No way!

Kathleen spoke openly about Sappho, as if they had been schoolmates, and told the women why she started the first school for women at a time in Greece's history when only men were educated. Though the school began as a center for teaching art, music, and poetry, it soon evolved into an underground forum for politics, philosophy, and the sciences. At the time, it would not have been considered proper for women to be involved in serious thought about anything outside the family and taking care of their husbands. Sappho was over twenty-five centuries ahead of her time. It was her goal to liberate women!

As each woman returned from their session with Kathleen and told her story, the excitement and anxious anticipation of the initiates waiting to meet with Kathleen heightened. No one was disappointed! When they returned, it was as if they had been gifted with a drug that would eliminate self-doubt, anxiety, and procrastination.

The initiates had become warriors for peace, change, and service to others. They would not quit until the battles were won. The war would be fought on the world stage against greed and exploitation from corporations and governments whose purpose was to misdirect, enslave, and control by making us afraid that without them we would not survive. While in truth, their policies and actions were the real threats to our survival, as well as that of our Mother Earth.

On a more local venue, the war would be brought to every home and neighborhood where people were experiencing the shame of poverty, the guilt of religions that preached, but did not practice, forgiveness and compassion, and the repression of some governments. It could not have been anticipated that these women, after their initiation, would be relentless in their efforts toward targeting the bullies of society in their many forms.

Before departing the stage, Kathleen had warned the audience that the final evening session on Sunday would include an initiation ceremony that would be beyond their wildest dreams. They would be introduced to activities never before witnessed in the history of our civilization—truly, an encounter beyond their present comprehension.

CHAPTER 12

Forgiveness

On Monday, the women were pampered, massaged and treated to fabulous cuisine. They spent time at the saunas and the pool, and some went shopping. After the dessert plates were removed from the tables at dinner, Kathleen took the stage. The room went quiet and the lights dimmed.

She began, "The first of our meetings will address your relationship with yourself and your family. Most of you are married. Regardless of your status, the happiness of those around you will be profoundly affected by your happiness. It was no different during the time of Sappho. The happiness of the family was largely determined by the happiness of the wife or mother. Toward this end, Sappho would council her students to learn the secrets of self-awareness and self-improvement. She knew that the keystone for a strong society is the family and that the architect of family success and stability is strongly correlated with the attitudes and practices of the wife and mother.

To assist her students toward realizing their potential as students, workers, family members, and later, as wives, mothers or caretakers, Sappho took the time to assess, on a daily basis, her own behavior and each evening wrote a review of the day. Sappho addressed what she approved of or disapproved of, concerning her interactions with others. In essence, she took the time, as Socrates would later say, 'to know thyself'."

The women were focused and attentive, and eager for more!

She continued, "Starting tonight, before you read the story that will be given to you after my presentation, I want you to write down the events of your day and define those incidents with which you are pleased, as well as those with which you are uncomfortable in any way. It is in the review and confrontation of your discomfort that you will ask the questions, and later find the answers, that will bring about your ongoing evolution as a person, wife or parent. Upon returning to your room, you will find a book on your desk that has been provided for this purpose. It is for you to keep and for your eyes only.

The stories each evening, aside from guiding you to think in new or novel ways, have been written by a man who, like me, completed an initiation process with the Gifted One. The topics covered will address a variety of important self-actualization concepts critical for your development and provide you with seeds of thought that, if properly cultivated, will enhance your ability to make needed changes in yourself, and will also empower you to inspire and motivate others.

Remember that change does not occur overnight but rather, is the result of consistent choices directed toward a specific purpose or goal. When enough good choices are made by enough people, the group consciousness of a society moves toward a tipping point. When that tipping point has been realized, there can be no turning back because a perception has evolved that makes the old way, or old perception, obsolete.

For example, there was a time when it was funny when someone drank too much alcohol and acted in an intoxicated manner. It's not funny now! Also, there was a time when making fun of folks who had any one of a variety of physical or mental handicaps was perceived as humorous. That too has changed.

Your challenge tonight is to determine the relationship forgiveness plays in your life in regard to family, friends, co-workers and yourself. If there is ever a chance to bring about world peace, it will only occur when the hatred for others, who are perceived as inferior, untrustworthy or villainous, is replaced, where appropriate, with acceptance.

THE POWER OF FORGIVENESS!

by City Bear

Muriel was every parent's nightmare: vicious, strong willed, intimidating and ruthless. Alice was eleven when Muriel, the unsanctioned fifth-grade boss, decided that Alice would be the target of her bully tactics. She would do her best to destroy Alice, even though Alice had never harmed her in any way. She wanted to destroy her simply for the fun of it.

Muriel had decided that Alice would be a good target because she was shy and easy to bully. So, Muriel got her posse together at the lunch table where all the "in" girls sat. She told them that Alice's clothes were really stupid and the way she wore her hair was hideous. Therefore, she did not deserve to be considered human and definitely not spoken to.

Muriel made it clear that if any of her female classmates spoke to Alice they too would be shunned. It scared the bejesus out of them. For a girl, being shunned in fifth grade was the equivalent of being sentenced to death. Many would say it was worse because after an execution, it's over; not so with being shunned.

Alice's mother and father were having a difficult time financially and her clothes and shoes were usually hand-me-downs from older cousins. She didn't have any brothers or sisters.

D-Day! On the day that Muriel proclaimed Alice should be shunned, she carried out the dastardly deed by inviting her to the lunch table where the firing squad awaited. Alice sat down and smiled at the other girls and, when no one smiled back, she knew something was wrong.

Muriel spoke, "Alice, we've decided that your clothes are funky and stupid and we don't like you. We're not going to speak to you! You don't exist! You're a nothing!"

Alice was stunned. It was as if she was struck with a Taser gun. She didn't answer and all the girls got up, walked away, and left her sitting alone at the table. When the realization set in as to what had happened, she just sat there and cried.

Muriel, seeing Alice's condition, made a joke about it to the girls, now sitting three tables away, and they all laughed.

For the rest of the day, Alice had no idea what her teachers were saying. In all her classes, everything seemed to be happening in slow motion and she had to do everything in her power to keep from fainting. All she could think about was telling her mom.

Daniel hated his father. In fact, many times a day he would say, "I hate him!" He hated him because he never knew him and felt unloved and rejected. His dad went to jail when he was just shy of his second birthday. That was ten years ago; his father was due to be released within a week.

Daniel's father sent him cards for his birthday, Christmas, special events, and sometimes just to say that he was thinking of him. He also sent what little money he could from earnings saved from working in the prison laundry. He loved Daniel more than life itself, and if God presented him with the ultimatum that either he or his son would have to die that day, there would be no hesitation, he would spare his son!

The knock on the door came just after dinner, about 6:20 p.m., and Daniel knew who it was. Rarely did anyone come to visit. When they did, friends and family just walked in; no one knocked. He told himself that he had nothing to say to his father; he was a criminal who had left him alone for ten years. He had robbed a store, got caught, and received the punishment he deserved. End of story! For ten years, when the other kids talked about doing things with their dads, it was too painful to listen and he walked away.

Standing six feet two and weighing two hundred and ten pounds, his father looked impressive. He had opened the door and stood at the doorway holding a small suitcase in one hand and a cap in the other. Despite his stature, he seemed like a little boy standing before the school principal, not knowing what would happen.

Daniel's mom, Mary, rushed over to her husband and hugged him. Embracing, they cried as Daniel walked away to his room and locked the door.

The next day, and for weeks thereafter, Daniel avoided his father. He never looked at him or spoke to him. His father never pushed it. While incarcerated, patience was something he had to practice every day, and in his daily prayers, he asked the Lord to let him know the right time to speak to his son.

Daniel's mom had become increasingly upset about the cold war going on in her home and finally, after weeks of tension, while his dad went for a walk, she asked Daniel to sit with her at the kitchen table. After all the years of keeping the secret, she decided to tell him the story.

She told him that when he was almost two, he was very sick and there was no money for a doctor. They took him to the Emergency Room and could see by the crowd of people waiting that it would take hours for them to see the doctor. She explained that she went to tell the nurse in charge that her child was having trouble breathing; the nurse told her she had to wait her turn.

His mom continued, "Your dad heard the nurse's directive and so he went to her and pleaded to have you seen. She was even nastier to your father; after berating him for his impatience, she looked at him with annoyance and walked away. Your father walked out without saying a word. He went to a nearby convenience store, acted like he had a gun in his pocket and told the cashier that he wanted all the money in the register. He got one hundred and fifty-one dollars. He walked back to the hospital, gave me the money, and took us around the corner to the doctor where we had to pay. Because your father was recognized on the store camera, the police came to the house later in the day and arrested him. That's the story you didn't know!"

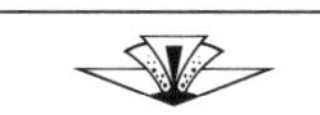

Alice was terrific in English and her teacher, seeing her crying alone at the lunch table, asked her to join her in her room. Mrs. Snyder always ate lunch by herself and told Alice that the teachers' room was toxic; too much complaining. Mrs. Snyder didn't ask Alice why she was crying; she figured she would tell her when she was ready. Alice was still in shock during her lunch with Mrs. Snyder. She couldn't speak! The next day, she asked Mrs. Snyder if she could have lunch with her again and it became their routine for the rest of the year. All the teachers knew what had happened.

Alice and Mrs. Snyder were becoming friends and, as the year progressed, Mrs. Snyder began to think of her as the daughter she never had.

It didn't take long for Alice to tell Mrs. Snyder the story she already knew. She asked Alice if she could speak to Muriel, but Alice said it would only make matters worse. Thankfully, summer vacation arrived and the pressure was off until September.

Alice dreaded the first day of school and the anxiety of having to cope with Muriel and company. As it is with life, everything has a beginning, middle, and end, and Muriel's reign of terror was about to end.

Over a month went by after Daniel's talk with his mother and he still told himself that he hated his father. The feeling of tension in the house was palpable; there was no peace, joy or comfort. Daniel didn't care about the reason for his father's incarceration. His heart had turned to stone.

Daniel walked his friend Kiera home from school on a Friday afternoon. Kiera was special! She was the type who made friends with kids who were handicapped or "not cool." She was an avid reader, wrote aphorisms that demonstrated wisdom beyond her age, and was an outstanding track athlete. She was also very pretty!

On the walk home, it was overcast and looked like it might rain any minute. Kiera sensed that something was wrong and asked Daniel about it. He told her the story. She listened!

She didn't respond for what seemed like an eternity for Daniel. Then she said, "Your father loves you more than he cares about himself. He was willing to get shot by the store owner or go to jail, rather than watch you die. I'm sorry he was away for so long and I know you feel cheated. Sometimes, circumstances make people do things they wouldn't ordinarily do!

It's easy to make decisions about other people based on what we know is for sure, even though most times what we know is incomplete. When we hear the whole story, things can be seen very differently! You need to forgive your dad for him and also, for you!" Then she walked up the steps to her house before Daniel could respond.

Alice had no idea that things were about to change dramatically. Marcy had transferred from a posh, private school in Massachusetts. She was tall, thin, blonde, and rich and a sociopath: no conscience or empathy and a fascination with cruelty. It was like a drug for her. She found it euphoric.

She sized up the sixth grade class hierarchy during the first week of school and crafted her plan; she would annihilate Muriel. She started by spreading rumors about Muriel having sex with some of the boys and followed it up with horrific anonymous Facebook comments. Muriel was shaken by this, and, realizing her groundwork had been successful, Marcy invited Muriel and her posse to her lunch table. She acted really sweet.

When everyone was seated, the show began. She told Muriel she was a slut and she went on and on. When Muriel fought back, it was no contest. Marcy had lined up her ducks and was ready for anything Muriel said. She had intimidated the girls to the point where some were actually shaking. She advised them that if they spoke to Muriel or, hung out with her, they'd pay for it—big time! She told them to leave the table and they did. Muriel looked like she was going to cry as Marcy walked away. During the next week any of the girls that remained close to Muriel were "spoken to" by Marcy. By the end of the week, Muriel was sitting at the lunch table by herself.

Alice passed by the lunch room on her way to Mrs. Snyder's and saw Muriel sitting alone. She had heard about the massacre. When she walked toward Muriel, her old enemy started to cry and put her hands over her face. Between the sobs, Muriel said, "I'm so sorry! I'm so sorry! Can you ever forgive me?"

Alice didn't respond. Instead, she said, "Would you like to join me? I'm having lunch with Mrs. Snyder, my English teacher."

They had lunch with Mrs. Snyder for the rest of the year and during that time Alice learned that Muriel's father was physically abusive to her, and that her mother had a severe alcohol problem. She had become a bully because her parents had taught her well! The following September, Alice and Muriel moved on to junior high. There, they continued their relationship and formed a bond that would last forever. Twelve years later, when Alice was married, Muriel was her maid of honor.

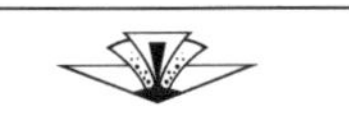

Daniel's father had been looking for a job without success. He felt broken, alone, and without hope when Daniel came in from his walk with Kiera. Something magical had happened in the short time it took for Daniel to walk home. Kiera's words had softened his heart. As his father sat at the kitchen table, Daniel saw him for the first time for what he really was: a dad who loved him enough to give up his freedom for him.

When their eyes met, Daniel began to cry. So did his father. He hugged his dad and, between sobs, said, "I love you, Daddy! I'm sorry!"

His father replied, "I love you too, son!"

Alice and Daniel came from very different places and with very different people, and yet, they shared common ground because they found it in their hearts to forgive. Mrs. Snyder and Kiera played pivotal roles in the process.

As it says in the Bible, "Those who forgive will be forgiven." What it doesn't say is that forgiveness can also bring release from bondage stronger than any chain!

CHAPTER 13

The Calling

By dinner time on Tuesday, eight of the women had been seen individually by Kathleen and each of them were enthusiastic about sharing their experience. All of them mentioned the glasses which allowed Kathleen to see things about themselves that they denied or outright rejected. However, the manner in which she presented her recognitions, and the examples she gave of events or interactions were on the mark. Every woman was amazed and stated openly that the one hour spent with Kathleen provided insights and suggestions that were life-altering.

As was customary, Kathleen took the stage after dinner. She wore the same sparkling white tunic she wore the night before and more than one woman remarked that she didn't have to worry about what she was going to wear!

Kathleen began, "Each of us has a calling; something that you are on Earth to do. Sometimes you may be very clear about what it is and other times, you might be guided or directed at some pivotal point in your life. For some people, this may be a tragedy, and for others, just the simple decision to follow one's heart regardless of the risk or potential consequences."

Again, she touched a nerve. The women were totally focused without movement or whispering.

"It is my hope that your involvement and actions this week will help you to determine your calling. To do so, I suggest that every day you spend some time alone in silence, and focus on the rose provided for each of you in your room. Sit quietly, focus on the petals and look into its heart. Look at the rose as if nothing else exists in your world and take time to slow your mind and listen to the revelations that accompany the silence.

"You might think it was very different during Sappho's time. However, it is always the same. There was too much to do and not enough time. There were worries and problems, usually related to money and relationships. Many women had few opportunities outside the home, and the general belief was that women should not be educated. It was through education that Sappho decided to follow her passion and provide an opportunity for girls to have the same opportunity as boys. As I am sure you can imagine, her decision was not accepted with open arms and support."

The women were captured in the moment by Kathleen's words; no one thought of speaking or interrupting. They were assessing themselves and wondering about their calling. Each woman had begun a self-evaluation process that would continue for the rest of the week.

"The story provided for you tonight is about a woman who thought that she was quite ordinary. As will happen with many of you, you will be given signs and guidance concerning your calling. It is your decision to further assess your mission on Earth and to make the decision that is right for you. Only you can decide. The story this evening was written to remind you of the difference one person can make. Especially if that person believes with all her heart and soul that she, and she alone, has been put on this planet for a specific reason.

"My challenge, this evening, is to use the information provided by me in our individual session and combine it with what you learn during the week. Practice the rose exercise daily and give yourself the freedom to think in ways that may presently seem foreign to you."

JUST A FOURTH GRADE TEACHER

by City Bear

Maureen McKenna was fourteen when she fell in love with Christ. Is that possible? Does a fourteen-year old girl know what love really is? In her case, there was no doubt. Her dream was to become a Sister of Charity.

Her parents didn't want to hear about it. Her father was especially opposed and would not discuss the possibility. Though she dated during her teenage years, she knew that as soon as she was old enough to make her own decision about her vocation, she'd become a nun.

As with many dreams that are focused and acted upon, she became a novice and eventually took her final vows. Mom and dad were not happy. They wanted a marriage and grandchildren; however, there was far more in store for Maureen than they could ever dream. In time, she would bring the hierarchy of the Catholic Church to their knees.

The years passed and she taught fourth grade at Our Lady of Mercy Elementary School in Cleveland, Ohio. Everyone loved her, even the difficult older sisters who felt she was not holy enough. She liked to have an occasional beer, sometimes two, and sing and play guitar. She was also funny—mostly self-deprecating humor that would make even the crabbiest among the sisters laugh.

Twenty years quickly passed and everything had changed. Very few of the sisters had stayed on the job. Most left and got married or found another vocation. Many felt they were second-class citizens in the eyes of the Church and could not—or would not—accept it. They wanted to be recognized for what they were: equal to men.

Her epiphany would take place on a wintry Friday evening

when the folks she usually spent time with had other commitments. It was very unusual: a Friday night when she was alone. She decided to spend the time in meditation and prayer—not what most forty-year olds would think of as a good time.

Maureen sat at her desk and looked at her watch. The time was exactly 7:09 p.m. She closed her eyes and began a form of transcendental meditation that she had learned many years before: she took a deep breath and silently repeated her mantra, I-Ma, over and over. She could feel her body beginning to relax when the voice that started as a whisper, beyond her ability to hear clearly, became louder and distinct. The voice was the most beautiful one she had ever heard. Filled with love, it also exuded power and confidence. It was female! It was calming, reassuring, and overwhelming. The speaker's tone commanded attention; full attention!

Within a very short time, she was given instructions. Instructions to change the Catholic Church, the wealthiest, and some say, the most powerful organization in the world. It was made clear that her new job would take her far beyond the classroom to center stage in a world arena. As she listened, she shook her head left to right indicating her conscious belief that the assignment was beyond her. She responded, "I'm a teacher; a fourth grade teacher. I wouldn't have the slightest idea where to begin."

The voice answered, "Start by running for U.S. Senate. The seat is open because the man who held it passed over. The position is waiting for you."

"Senate?" she queried. And the voice continued, "You will be guided. You are being empowered to do things in this world that are long overdue. Your faith, hope, and continued charity are the only shields you need to protect you from all obstacles and challenges." The voice stopped.

Maureen looked at her watch. Exactly one hour had passed since she had begun her meditation. It seemed like ten minutes, but she felt exhausted. The idea was overwhelming. A religious sister who would change the Catholic Church? Doubt crept into her psyche like a thief in the night and she had to remind herself that she would be guided. The words "faith, hope, and charity" kept ringing in her mind—she could not flip the switch to turn off the recording. She decided to say a rosary, hoping it would calm her, and it did, but it did not stop the words from repeating: "faith, hope, and charity."

She went to her bookshelf and her eyes were immediately drawn to a book on the top shelf. It was a book she had never read. In fact, she couldn't even remember who had given her the book it was that long ago. The book, with a golden fleur-de-lis on the cover, was titled: The Life of Joan of Arc. Immediately, she knew who the voice belonged to! She felt an overwhelming sense of power, peace, and commitment. She knew, without the slightest doubt, that she had been visited by St. Joan of Arc.

She told her Mother Superior that she planned to run for the U.S. Senate and her response was very clear, "Absolutely not!"

Maureen didn't want to explain the voice, the instructions, nor the book. She thought she would be laughed at. Mother Superior continued, "Your job is to serve, and my job is to tell you that politics is out of the question!"

This is not going to be a ride in the park, she thought. *More likely, I'm sitting in the front seat of a roller coaster and tightening my seat belt!*

She did run for Senate and won, and the Mother Superior became her most ardent supporter. Maureen was a powerhouse. She was more than a breath of fresh air. She was a hurricane that swept away anything in its path with directness, fairness, and an obvious desire to serve others. Her humor about politics and politicians rivaled Will Rogers. There was even talk about making a movie of her life. Unimpressed, Maureen continued to arise at 5 a.m. and work most days until midnight.

A year had passed until one morning, while meditating, the voice returned. At first, it frightened her. Again, it started as an inaudible whisper, and then she heard the command, "Let the peace of the Lord be with you!" With these words, all fear and doubt were swept aside. She felt invincible.

The voice continued, "We have a new Pope and he's a good man; however, to do what needs to be done will require grassroots movement never seen before in the history of the Church. You will use your influence and popularity to lead and guide."

The old demons of doubt returned. Immediately, the silent voice reassured her and said, "If you have faith the size of a mustard seed..." And Maureen finished the quote in her mind.

You will do the following, the voice commanded: "In your speaking engagements around the country, you will suggest that the Pope sell the Vatican treasures to support and develop programs for the poor; second, you will also suggest that in the Catholic Church women be given the same rights and advantages as men. This includes becoming priests. You will also reinforce what the Pope has said about gay men and women...that Christ loves them, as he loves all of us. Therefore, they should have the same rights as all people. You will also suggest that people who are divorced and remarry are no longer excommunicated but rather, welcomed back to the Church. Finally, you will suggest that members of the church hierarchy remove their outdated costumes—especially the hats—and wear plain white cassocks."

Maureen's breathing had become faster with each suggestion until finally, she said, "This is way beyond me!"

The voice responded, "Mustard seed!"

"But how?" asked Maureen desperately.

"By remembering the power of the sacred feminine, you will advise women in the United States, as well as around the world, that if the Church does not make the needed changes, women will no longer attend church or be involved in any of her activities."

The groundswell began slowly. There was ferocious pushback from the church hierarchy, including the Pope. The women were relentless. In the spirit of Gandhi and Dr. King, their protest was totally non-violent. No one even raised their voice. They began their silent protest by not attending church. Sunday attendance by women dropped to fifty percent and later, seventy percent. The reduction in contributions became a constant concern for the hierarchy. The Church was falling apart!

Then, there was the call. "Sister Maureen, this is Father Vincent Boliglio, the representative to His Holiness at the Vatican. I have been directed to contact you and request that you clear your schedule to meet with His Holiness at 10:00 a.m. on September 22. All flight accommodations and room reservations will be taken care of through my office and you will receive all the necessary documents in the mail within a week from today. Do you have any questions?"

Maureen was in shock! Everything seemed to move in slow motion and her mouth and throat had become dry. She swallowed, took a deep breath and responded, "There must be some mistake, are you sure you have the right Sister Maureen? I mean you're saying the Pope wants to speak with me?"

The voice on the other end of the phone made a breathy sigh, suggesting that he understood her consternation. He said with a wisp of an Italian accent, "Yes, Sister Maureen, there is no mistake. His Holiness needs to speak with you!"

"Is there something wrong?" Maureen asked, knowing full well that she was the force behind the decrease in attendance and financial contributions.

No answer! Then, he repeated, "You will receive the documents and directions you need in the mail. May the peace of the Lord be with you!" And the phone went silent.

With her heart pounding and her hands shaking, she walked to Mother Superior's room and knocked. There was no answer, so she knocked again. Silence!

She thought, *Maybe the chapel?* She was right. Mother was kneeling before the Blessed Sacrament in prayer. When the door opened, she turned and, seeing Maureen, invited her to come forward. They sat together in the front pew, and Maureen told her the story, hoping for some comfort and advice.

Mother responded, "You're frightened, Maureen, aren't you?"

"Yes!"

"Maureen, do you believe the Lord wants you to do what you're doing?"

"Yes!"

"Then hold your head high and meet with His Holiness and remember that anything worthwhile is scary. Think of our Lord in the garden. He asked if the crucifixion could be taken from Him. He was frightened, but he accepted His Father's will and did what needed to be done. I will pray for you, Maureen, and I will ask all of the sisters to do so!"

On the appointed day and time, Maureen met with the Pope. Father Boliglio escorted her to the conference room and asked her to be seated. Less than five minutes later, the door opened and His Holiness walked toward her with his right hand outstretched. She stood and went to kiss the ring on his finger but he covered it with his left hand.

"Maureen, I want to shake your hand." As she shook his hand, he put his left hand over both their hands and smiled at her—a smile that would be locked in her mind forever. She knew he was not angry. She knew everything would be okay. She knew his heart resonated with the love of Christ and whatever happened would be fine with her.

He said, "Please sit. Maureen, I suspect you think I am angry with you because of what has happened in the Church in the United States as a result of your meetings around the country. I'm not angry, instead, I am grateful. What you have asked for, I agree with. Without the women's protest, the pushback I would get from the bishops would be overwhelming. Now, because of you and the women of the United States, they realize change must happen and happen quickly."

Maureen felt as if she were floating. She thought, *Is this real? The Pope has just thanked me for causing insurrection!*

As if he could read her thoughts, he smiled and continued, "There is much more for you to do, Maureen! The Vatican treasures will be sold and the money used to educate the poor, so that they will be able to lift themselves from poverty. I would like you to be in charge of selling the treasures and dispensing the funds. The focus of your work will be to provide the poor with the skills they need to survive and thrive. In the beginning, you will give these people fish, but in time, you will teach them to fish."

His Holiness stood and, as he did, Maureen arose and went to kiss his ring. Again, he covered the ring with his left hand. This time, as he shook her hand, he turned it palm down and kissed the back of her hand. He smiled and while walking back to his quarters said,

"Maureen, arrangements are being made to have all your belongings brought to the Vatican. We have the Lord's work to do!"

Coincidentally, on the feast day of St. Joan of Arc, the Pope stood at his balcony in the Vatican, wearing a plain white cassock, and told the awaiting multitude below that he had decided to make long overdue changes in the Church that would bring about changes in the world. He started by inviting all Catholics who had been divorced and remarried to come back to the Church. The applause started. He continued by telling the crowd about his love for all people, including those who are gay. The applause increased as he spoke about the need to sell the Vatican treasures and to feed and educate the poor. He told the crowd that it was time for women to have the same rights as men in the church, which included becoming priests. The applause was deafening.

Finally, realizing his message had been heard, and because the cheering crowd would not allow anyone to hear his final words, the Pope decided to simply make the sign of the cross in blessing the thousands before him. He turned, and the doors of the balcony were closed.

Maureen had been in the crowd. She wanted to be with the people to witness and hear the words of the Pope from the common man or woman's perspective. The Pope's message was by far the most powerful experience of her life and as the doors to the balcony closed she thought, *If you have faith the size of a mustard seed....*

CHAPTER 14

The Choice

By Wednesday, the group had ventured deeply into the process of becoming more than a collection of individuals. They were evolving into a caring, cooperative, and functioning unit with a desire to work together to bring about change in themselves. And some of the people already had a burning desire to bring about change on a grander scale—the world.

Tonight Kathleen's tunic wasn't white. It was royal blue and more than one woman wanted to buy a similar garment when they returned home or maybe even in one of the local stores. Her hair was styled in a French braid and she wore a matching blue scarf that gave the tunic a touch of sophistication. The women wondered if the change in the color of her tunic meant anything. It became a topic for discussion. The truth be known, some of her clothes had been misdirected to another hotel suite and had not been available until Wednesday morning.

She began, "The process of change starts with a decision. That decision requires a choice and most people don't really decide to make changes unless they have enough pain. Think of an alcoholic or a drug addict. They don't change until they hit bottom. I ask all of you to think of what you want to change about yourself. Something that has eluded you in spite of your 'trying.' The truth is that 'trying' is deciding not to change. Trying is an excuse that allows you to feel good about not changing."

Once again, she had them. They wanted more and they wanted answers. An approach, a plan that would bring about desired results.

Kathleen continued, "Our lives and the problems and challenges we face were determined long before we were born. They represent the key concepts in our life curriculum and, in the end, we grade ourselves. In every case, the pass or fail grade is determined by our ability to step outside our comfort zone and take an action, based on a choice about which we feel uncomfortable. It might mean deciding to start or end a relationship. It could involve taking a risk about a new job or moving to another town or city and maybe starting your own business. For some people, it can be as simple as saying what is in your heart and demanding respect from someone who has taken you for granted or abused you."

The soul searching was in full bloom and as Kathleen looked into the faces of the women, it was obvious she had touched a nerve; maybe many nerves.

"It was no different during the time of Sappho!—unrequited love; relationships that no longer were satisfying; children who disappointed their parents; family feuds; jobs that provided little or no reward, and most of all, the feeling of being trapped in a variety of situations with no way out. Do any of these situations sound familiar?"

There were no words from the women but many were nodding their heads in recognition of Kathleen's truths.

"Sappho was in the same position as many of you. She was a brilliant woman at a time when women were often seen as property. She wanted to fulfill her destiny and live out her dreams. In order to do, she had to disregard the advice that the climate of the time and well-meaning family and friends offered. In essence, she had to chart her own course and make decisions that defied logic and advice. She was a trailblazer and was thought of by many to be the grandmother of the women's movement. Her decision to start a school for girls is honored today because she made a choice, took action and, most importantly, thought outside the parameters of the time. Today, we call it thinking 'outside the box.'

"To bring about changes in your life and to do your part in bringing about needed changes in the world, thinking outside the box for answers is a requirement. Why? Because what has been done so far has not worked. Our world is controlled by banks, corporations, individuals, and leaders whose goals are not aligned for the betterment of mankind but rather for greed, control, and power. Overwhelmingly, the people in the seats of power are men with very few women involved. That must and will change!

"Tonight's story is about a family and the presentation of a situation that would incite the wrath of any mother or father. It provides an example of thinking 'outside the box' by a mother whose love for her daughter incited the development and execution of a plan that provided justice when it seemed that nothing could be done to rectify an egregious wrong. The story will awaken your thinking and dismiss the idea and acceptance that there are no answers to problems."

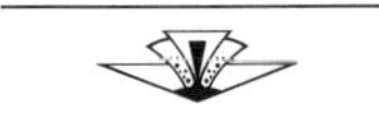

THE CRUELEST JOKE

by City Bear

Seated in her living room, Anna fidgeted in her prom dress, waiting for the bell to ring. It never did. At first, she was worried that maybe something had happened to him. After the phone call from her friend, she realized she was the target of a joke that could only be described as life-alteringly cruel.

Miles Murray III was handsome, funny, the captain of the high school football team, and a sociopath. His relationship with Anna started with a bet. Miles and Drew Preminger were having lunch in the high school cafeteria when Anna walked in. At five feet four inches tall and one hundred and sixty pounds, she was not a Homecoming Queen candidate. As she waddled to the cashier with her salad and diet Coke, the whole idea unfolded for Drew: the perfect practical joke and maybe the meanest.

They watched Anna pay for her lunch and when she walked by their table Drew said, "Hey Anna! Great answer in class today!" Anna was a chemistry whiz and the teacher had asked the class a question to which only Anna offered an answer. And she was right. She didn't like Drew, although he wouldn't have known that. She was kind and polite to everyone; even the people whom she figured made fun of her behind her back. Drew was one of those!

After she passed, Drew said to Miles, "Why don't you ask her to the prom?"

Miles looked at Drew as if he had just stepped in a big pile of dog crap and with a frown said, "Why don't you ask her? You just told her how smart she is?"

"Okay! Here's the bet," Drew said. "I'll bet you a hundred bucks you can't get her to go to the prom with you!"

Miles said, "D, you know I'm going to the prom with Sandy. Everybody knows!"

Drew replied, "That's it! Suppose we spread the rumor that you and Sandy broke up and you need a date for the prom, but you need to start now."

Miles said, "What d'ya mean, start now?

Drew said, "You're lousy in chemistry and if you fail, you're off the football team. Call Anna and ask her if she'll tutor you. It's a 'win-win' for you."

"How is it a win-win?" asked Miles.

Drew responded, "She's really smart and she'll help you pass. It'll be a big deal for her and you make like you're falling in love with her. Touch her hand and face and look at her like she's you're dream come true. Nobody wants her, so she won't be able to help herself. She'll be your toy and the best is yet to come."

Miles said, "What d'ya mean, 'the best is yet to come'?"

Drew responded, "You're gonna need her for basketball season. Chemistry is two semesters. Again, she'll help you pass. By now, she's dreaming about you and writing Mr. and Mrs. Miles Murphy III over and over on a lined yellow pad. She'll be salivating like that dog they talked about in psych class when it heard the bell, even though there was no meat powder. When you ask her to the prom, she'll wet her pants."

Miles said, "I'm not convinced D, anyway, there's no friggin' way I'm takin' her to the Junior prom."

Drew answered, "That's the joke! Everyone will know but her. She sits there waiting for you and you go to the prom with Sandy. It'll be a hoot! Everybody will crack up. It's the ultimate goof on the smart kid."

Drew continued, "A hundred bucks! I know I'm betting against myself, but the laughs will be worth it. A hundred smackers says you can't pull it off!"

Miles said, "It's a deal!" And they shook hands to seal the contract having no idea of the power and ferocity of the animal to which they had just given birth. Certainly neither of them had heard saying: *Beware the wrath of a woman scorned!*

An hour had passed and there was still no Miles. Then the phone rang. It was Julia, Anna's best friend in school. Between her tears she said, "Those bastards, I don't believe they did this. Anna, Miles is here with Sandy. It was all a lie and a joke that's not funny. Arthur, my boyfriend, told me that Miles and Drew had a bet for one hundred dollars. Drew bet Miles that you would not go to the prom with him. He never intended to go; they just wanted to make fun of you and make you buy a dress and everything."

Anna felt sick to her stomach. She was on overload and needed to sit down. Then, just as she started to cry, her father came in.

Mr. Czerwinski was in his fifties, had emigrated from the Ukraine as a teenager, and had worked as a laborer in New York City for over thirty years. Mostly, he used a ninety pound jackhammer and moved it around like a loaf of bread. No effort! His forearms looked like the roots of an old tree and, after she told him what happened, he squeezed his fists so that the knots in his forearms looked like they were ready to explode.

He sat next to her and put his arms around her. She sobbed—that deep, gut wrenching sob that only comes with the greatest despair. Her dad was silent. After a few minutes, the crying became more controlled and Anna said, "I can't go back. I can't go back to school for my exams. I can't face them. I'd rather die. I don't care if I die. I've been such a fool!"

Her dad's breathing had started to slow down and he said, "Vee go home for summer. You vill see. Vee meet cousins and aunts and uncles. You vill see. You need change. New people, good people, who luf you!"

That night, she cried herself to sleep. The school sent a teacher to the house to give her the final exams for junior year, and the week after, Anna, her mother and father went home to the Ukraine.

The change was just what Anna needed. Her cousin, Svetlana, who met her at the airport and knew what had happened from her mother, Anna's mother's sister, and Svetlana, who had never met her cousin, was anxious with anticipation.

Svetlana was waiting with her mom and dad at the arrival grate holding a bouquet of flowers she had picked from their farm. She knew her aunt and uncle from family photos that had been shared and, when she saw Anna, she knew they would be friends forever. After she handed Anna the flowers, they hugged and both began to cry, oblivious to everyone around them.

Svetlana was physically everything Anna was not. She was cover-girl beautiful—tall, athletic and blonde—and in training for the Olympic decathlon.

On the way home in the car, the girls sat in the back with Anna's mother, while her uncle and father sat in the front. The conversation was cordial and Svetlana couldn't wait to get Anna alone. She had a plan and that night, over a campfire, she presented it to Anna. As she spoke, Anna could feel the depression lift, as if someone had removed a very heavy weight from her shoulders. By the end of the summer, Anna would become an athlete.

Up every morning at 4:30, and after the girls took care of their farm chores, they went for a run. At first, Anna could only jog less than one hundred yards. As the weeks passed, it became a quarter mile, then a mile, and by the time she returned to school, Anna was running five miles a day and had lost forty pounds. The afternoon gym workouts with Svetlana five days a week had also changed the shape of her body. Anna looked healthy and fit. Svetlana also taught her how to apply just the right amount of makeup—and the result was impressive. Anna had become a beautiful young woman.

The night before Anna and her parents were to return to the United States, Svetlana told her that she had a surprise for her and that she would know about it the following day. On the return trip to the airport, Svetlana's father announced that she would be going to America with Anna and her parents. She would live there for a year. They were both the same age, both seniors, and would both go to the same high school. Anna was deliriously happy with the news, and again, the tears were unleashed as she and her cousin hugged.

As with most events in the memory of teenagers, the prom debacle had a short lifespan, and in October, at a chance meeting in the school library, Miles told Anna that he was sorry, but he didn't mean it. He was motivated only by his desire to date Svetlana. Every guy in school was in love with her. In addition to her physical attributes, she was funny and charming. And the accent didn't hurt!

Anna saw it coming. Miles was as transparent as a clean window and she accepted his apology. Svetlana went out with Miles twice. He was only one conquest for her on an ever-lengthening list. The year passed and it came time for the senior prom. By this time, Miles was crazy for Svetlana and asked her to go with him. Anna had also been dating frequently and Drew, the demon seed who initiated the bet, had asked her out three times. He was interested, but not enchanted.

When Miles asked Svetlana to the prom, she said she'd go only if Drew went with Anna. Drew was more than interested in Cameron and had planned to ask her. Before he did, Miles pleaded with him to go with Anna. It was the only way Svetlana would go with him.

It was unfolding as Svetlana had planned. She told Miles that she and Anna would meet him and Drew at the prom at 7 pm. When the girls arrived, they had two tuxedo clad, handsome young men with them, Boris and Ivan Czerwinski, her cousins.

Miles and Drew were football players and physically outweighed Boris and Ivan by fifty pounds. At first they looked stunned, like someone had hit them with a bat. Then, angry! Drew began to use the f-word followed by a stream of obscenities in chorus with Miles.

Boris intervened, "Hey boyz! What did you haf for breakfast?"

Miles responded, "What do you care, Polock?"

Ivan answered, "Because you both haf egg on your face!"

Seeking redemption and feeling confident, Miles threw the first punch. It was blocked and answered by a straight left and a right hook that snapped like a whip. Miles was down and out.

Mr. Duffy, the English teacher, was standing next to the girls. He saw and heard everything.

Drew, taller and heavier than Miles, decided to throw a punch at Boris, the smaller of the two. No contest, Boris blocked the punch and his right cross response resulted in Drew being knocked cold and flat on his back.

The ambulance came first and then the police. The boys were taken to the hospital. When the questions started, Mr. Duffy explained that the Czerwinski boys had acted in self-defense.

There was no need to tell anyone that Miles and Drew had met Anna's cousins, the Ukrainian welterweight and middleweight boxing champions.

When told of the events the following day by Anna and Svetlana, Anna's father didn't say a word. Her mother, who had suggested the trip to the Ukraine, said, "To act in anger is to set to sea in storm. There is no vay you come out unscathed. Think before you act girls! Think before you act!"

Anna and her dad were never told that her mom had skillfully formulated and executed a plan whose conception was formulated in her kitchen while having a cup of tea. Svetlana was her accomplice. Her intent was to let the jokesters spring their own trap.

Although Anna and Svetlana would only see each other every few years, theirs had become a friendship that would stand the test of time.

CHAPTER 15

Willpower

Tonight, Kathleen's tunic was a golden yellow with a matching yellow and green-flowered scarf that was attractive in an understated way. Kathleen never mixed with the women during free time. Their only contact with her was during their one-hour individual session and the evening discourses. They loved her! She could have worn an old sackcloth for a dress and they would not have said an unkind or critical word. She had become their trusted friend and advisor.

"Good evening ladies! I hope your experience has been rewarding and restorative. My presentation tonight will focus on the power of your will to bring you to places about which you presently might only dream and to be involved in activities that currently seem far beyond you!

When Sappho was a girl, she was accused of being headstrong and stubborn. Her parents were often annoyed with her constant questioning of whatever crossed her path; when little more than a toddler, she began asking 'why' about almost everything. At first, her mother and father found it exhausting but, as her early years passed, they found her questioning stimulated their thinking. Because of her need to know the reasons for customs, practices, attitudes, and a wide variety of decisions, her parents began to reconsider much of what they had taken for granted. Her questions became the stimuli for their reassessment of the status quo!

Today, many people have become complacent and fail to ask important questions about their current and future lives. Questions like: Why does a tiny fraction of the population have most of the capital? Is it because they are much smarter or work harder? Why do many of the giant corporations, which make billions of dollars, pay little or no taxes? Why do we fight wars with other countries ostensibly to bring them democracy when they have not requested our intervention and have no idea what democracy means? Why do we allow our food to be genetically engineered when most of the world knows it's not healthy? Why have the number of vaccination shots for children from birth to six quadrupled in the last thirty years and the incidents of autism skyrocketed? Why have Americans allowed their government to get the country into so much debt? That's enough! By now, you understand my concern about asking the right questions."

The ladies looked visibly upset. The concern on their faces was obvious and the anxiety in the room was palpable. Kathleen's questions had touched nerves that could not be denied. One after the other, her questions had gained the momentum of a freight train barreling down the tracks. With each unanswered question, their discomfort increased because they knew she had brought them to a place where they had to face some very ugly and dangerous truths. Truths that were impacting them and everyone they loved, cared for, and cared about.

The tension broke when she said, "It doesn't have to be this way! You need to take back your power by demanding answers to your questions and holding people accountable. This is the age of the Sacred Feminine; a time in our history where the power of women is needed to challenge the patriarchal system and demand an equal voice in those decisions that affect everyone and everything on this planet.

"That equal voice will not happen unless you become involved in local, state, national, and international politics. It will only happen if, as I spoke yesterday, you feel enough pain to take action. Knowing how difficult it is for any of us to change, I ask each of you to decide the future you want for your children. If you take no action, our world will continue to spiral out of control and the futures for our children will be tragic beyond our current understanding.

"Much of what we are facing today was similar in the days of Sappho. She had the courage and conviction to ask questions that began a process whose power can be unleashed in your lifetime. As Gandhi, a thin, non-violent man who single-handedly brought Great

Britain to its knees remarked, 'Decide to be the change you want to see in the world.'

"It is my hope that tonight's story will provide an example that will ignite your involvement in local, state, national or international politics. Remember, to ask yourself the question, 'What do I want for the future of my children and what will I do to make it happen?'

"I believe in you, my sisters, and have confidence that each of you will make an important contribution that will enhance the future for all. I wish you pleasant dreams!"

There was something about tonight's presentation that was different. After each of Kathleen's talks on Monday, Tuesday, and Wednesday, the applause was loud and sustained. Tonight, it also included a standing ovation which brought Kathleen back to thank the women. She left the stage holding her right hand high and making the peace sign.

ERIN THE TERRIBLE

by City Bear

Erin Kathleen McCann entered the world with a mission. She wasn't a kid who had to be told what to do. Highly intelligent and intuitive, as a child she had it all figured out and sometimes her figuring clashed with the rules, but she never let the rules get in the way! There was a reason that at an early age her mom and dad called her "Erin the Terrible." A complex kid, sometimes she was sweet and charming and sometimes...ouch! Little would anyone suspect the mark she would eventually make on the great state of Texas. A mark that would change things forever.

Standing just over five feet and weighing just a hundred and five pounds, as a senior, she was a mini powerhouse, and after graduation from Abilene High, was accepted at Texas A&M University as a business major. Wherever she went, she left a trail of fairy dust. She knew instinctively what to say, and with her sweet Texas drawl, she could charm the skin off a rattlesnake. Amazing! She was something to watch and the folks who got to know her, more than once thought, *That girl is going somewhere!*

It didn't take long for her to recognize that she disliked college. It was boring! Following someone else's lead was not for her. She could have graduated *summa cum laude*, but she dropped out and decided to get her license as a hairstylist. She worked her art and it didn't take long for folks to recognize her talent.

The ladies would wait for her, even before she became the owner of her own salon. She was a female version of Bill Clinton in her ability to read folks and speak to them in a manner that made them feel they were best friends, even though they had just met.

Born on a ranch, her dad was a school teacher and her mom, a housekeeper. She had an older brother and sister. When she was in high school a "Land Man" came to the door and asked to speak to her mom and dad. He wanted them to sign a lease for their one hundred acre farm, so that his company could drill for natural gas.

Her parents would receive a fourteen percent royalty for the product pumped. At the time, many folks had them but nothing had happened with these leases for over thirty years. Gas wells were very uncommon. Her parents decided to sign and received a stipend of thirty-five dollars for each acre. Nine years went by before the "Land Man" returned and explained that his company had decided to drill the following spring.

By that time, Erin was working for a salon chain when her dad phoned and told her about the proposed drilling. The dangers of fracking, pumping high pressure water into the well to separate the gas from the rock, had been widely recognized and discussed on radio and TV. Mom and dad never expected that a dream which started as a promise of unexpected wealth might turn into a nightmare. The water that had sustained them and their animals, after the fracking started, became undrinkable. It smelled like rotten eggs. And the fourteen percent royalty shrunk to one and a half percent because of additional charges that the gas company included, and which were legal because of the convoluted legal language in the lease document.

It appeared that nothing could be done. The gas company not only had the signed lease, they also controlled the local and state politicians and had unlimited resources to fight any lawsuit brought against them. All seemed lost with no way out.

In addition to being gifted intellectually, Erin was an artist—a painter, sculptor, writer, and had a real talent for cutting and styling men's and women's hair. In high school, she started cutting her friends' hair and became so popular that her dad converted part of their garage into a small shop where neighbors and friends came to get a cut, style or color. She loved chemistry in high school and it made her a natural for coloring the ladies' hair. At that time, it was uncommon in Abilene, at least, for men to color their hair.

When her parents began having the problems with the gas company, Erin had a few years' experience as a licensed hairstylist and barber. After graduation, she worked for an upscale chain salon for five years before she opened her own business in town. Within a year, she had to hire four people to help her. She had the magic! She charmed men, women, and children to the point where, once they came through the door, chances of getting a cut or style elsewhere were unlikely. It wasn't the cut or style; going to her shop was an experience and folks left covered with invisible fairy dust—the stuff of which Erin seemed to have an unlimited supply!

Mom and Dad felt they had been ripped off by the gas company and no one seemed to be able or willing to help. One of Erin's customers suggested that the only way to get anything accomplished was to become involved in politics. He said, "The election for governor is this year. Why not give it a try?"

Never one to shy away from a challenge, she did, and was the only female on the ballot. She was also the only Independent running. There were two Republicans and one Democrat in the race. The following three debates were hilarious, as long as you weren't one of her opponents. When she first announced her candidacy, the media ridiculed her. Headlines like: "Lady Barber Wants to Cut Spending!" and, "Lady Clipper wants to be Skipper!" No one thought she had a chance; no one except her mom, dad, and her husband. They thought, *Her opponents have no idea what they're in for!*

When asked questions about the state's economy, Erin was knowledgeable and practical. She knew where the fat was in the budget and who was getting more than their fair share. She told it how she saw it, and folks saw her as a breath of fresh air. After the first debate, donations started to roll in and the other candidates stopped laughing. Everyone was talking about her. She spoke at schools, hospitals, nursing homes, and any group that would allow her to explain why she should be governor.

On the day she announced her candidacy, her husband began looking into the contracts that had been awarded for the last four years by the current governor. He found more than enough ammunition to sink his political ship. He also found out that another candidate had a huge gambling problem and had borrowed money from people who were allegedly connected to the Mob. The final candidate, Jeff learned, was involved in the development of a shopping center where the land had been bought far below the market value from a Native American tribe whose council president had been indicted by the FBI.

For the second debate, the TV stations recorded the highest viewer ratings in their history. It seemed as if everyone in Texas was watching Erin dismantle the old-boy network with facts, humor, and charm.

Little girls wanted the Erin hairstyle and some moms started to think that maybe, in some way, they could do what Erin was doing... challenge the establishment. She had become an inspiration—and not just to women. Men liked the way she handled tough questions without missing a step, while at the same time, making them laugh! For example, in one debate, an opponent, thinking that Erin would hold an anti-gun position, asked, "Do you believe that there are too many guns and that the NRA has too much power?"

She hesitated a few seconds and answered in a sweet Texas drawl, "Why Lloyd, just the other day, a man, who had been sent from the mayor of New York City, came into my shop. He told me that that, if I win the election, I would receive a very generous donation if I agreed to speak out against the NRA and support the gun grabbers." Then she stopped.

Lloyd continued, "What did you say?"

She looked over at Lloyd and in the most charming, feminine Texas drawl said, "I put down my scissors, went to the cash register's lower drawer where I keep my Smith and Wesson 357 Magnum revolver and showed him the gun. I told him if he didn't get out of my shop in five seconds, he'd be singing soprano in the church choir!"

The studio audience went wild. The laughter was so loud they had to wait for them to calm down before the next question could be asked.

After the folks learned about the crooked contracts, gambling, and crooked land deal issues, she won in a landslide. On the morning after the election, the Texas Star headline read: "Erin Scalps Her Opponents!"

Erin decided her first job as governor would be to meet with representatives from the oil and gas companies and convince them that it would be in their best interests to make it right: clean up the environment, fix the water problems, pay the agreed-upon royalty percentages and become good neighbors.

It didn't take long before Mom and Dad could drink the water again and receive their agreed-upon royalty checks.

And no one ever knew that behind this great woman was a great man, her husband, J.R.—a quiet man who was very willing to let his wife shine as brightly as she wished, as well as help her to do so.

Furthermore, the ladies of the great State of Texas having seen it done, began to take an interest in running for a wide variety of political offices that had been exclusively the domains of men. Erin the Terrible had become Erin the charming and finally, Erin the Governor. She never looked back. She had accomplished the impossible against competitors who had power and money. And she did it her way, with charm, intelligence, humor and a husband who loved a strong woman.

CHAPTER 16

Taking a Chance

On Friday night, Kathleen's tunic was a sea-foam green with a blue, green, and yellow-flowered scarf that was strikingly beautiful. Of all the outfits she wore, the women seemed to like this one best, making comments about it before she began to speak.

"I want to thank the women who have met individually with me for their honesty, integrity, and openness to my insights and suggestions. Theophane's choices have been magnificent and I am indebted to each of you for what you have taught me. I hope my time with you has been meaningful in your development as a woman and later as an agent of change.

It is not expected that all of you become politicians or world leaders, but what is expected is that you evolve to your highest potential. It is expected that, as Marianne Williamson advised, 'As we let our light shine, we unconsciously give other people permission to do the same. As we are liberated from our own fear, our presence automatically liberates others.'"

During their individual sessions with Kathleen, many women had expressed their anxiety about being able to meet her expectations. She used this opportunity to explain that she had no expectations other than what the women expected of themselves. She advised each of them to determine their strengths, as well as those areas they wanted to improve, and to use this formula for their development through life. She explained that they were all different, as the stars of the sky are different, and yet each has its own unique light. All of the women who met with Kathleen could not believe their hour with her went by so quickly and each agreed that their meeting was life-altering.

"Tonight's story is quite provocative because it involves a very controversial action completed with the highest good in mind, and yet, it is an action for which the woman involved could have been imprisoned. Remember ladies, all these stories presented are fictional. They have been designed by my colleague to provide you with unique approaches to complex problems. In this case, the actions taken by the heroine could be considered by most folks as being outside the law. I am not in any way condoning the action taken but simply presenting an unusual solution to a problem that remains very much unsolved."

The women were intrigued! There was murmuring in the audience, and it was the first time Kathleen had to wait for the women to become settled and quiet.

"Ladies, nothing really important ever gets accomplished without taking a chance. The woman in this story took a very big chance which had the potential to destroy her life. You may have heard it said that in order to be good, you have to obey the rules, but in order to be great, you have to know when to bend them. There is no question that the woman in the story bent the rules and, in the minds of many, broke them. However, in doing so, she brought about results that changed the lives of many.

"In closing, it is my fervent hope that, as a result of your involvement this week, your actions will validate a quote from Sappho, 'Even in an age unlike our own, someone will remember who we are.'"

DA-DA JONES

by City Bear

At the age of forty-three, Mom didn't want or need another child. There were seven already and it wasn't easy. Her husband drank too much and worked too little. She was born in Georgia and deeply religious, and being "old school," she didn't believe in divorce. She thought about terminating the pregnancy but just couldn't do it. She thought, *I'd always wonder about the child. How would he or she look? What would they become?* Consequently, she worked until her eighth month.

Tiffany, unlike her three brothers and four sisters, was born tiny. At five pounds two ounces, she was the smallest by far. And there was something wrong with her foot. They called it a clubfoot, for which she would have two operations. No one suspected she would have a speech impediment that would eventually cause her overwhelming pain and embarrassment.

Mom worked two jobs and, when available, a third, cleaning up the church after services on Sunday. She worked for a big insurance firm in Manhattan and never missed a day of work, except for the final month of each pregnancy. She loved the job and the folks there loved her. At Christmas, each year, she received cards and presents from the office workers and they always called her Mrs. J., not Ethel, her given name. Her demeanor and work ethic had won their respect. She often spoke about the day when she would be able to retire and collect her pension. It kept her going. The thought of being able to finally relax gave her comfort.

When Tiffany was three, her mom noticed that her speech was not as developed as her other children at that age, and she seemed to stutter; she would say the beginning sound of a word two or three times before blurting out the word. She was also very quiet and spent most of her time playing with her brother's old computer. She was five-years old when she started with the computer and, when in second and third grade, she was able to help her teachers with computer questions. She was amazing! She wasn't just bright; she was brilliant and all the teachers talked about her.

Like many exceptional people, her gift came with a price. Because she wasn't tall and beautiful like her sisters who were outgoing and popular, Tiffany retreated into the world of her computer. She was never a problem in school until she was asked in second grade to read for the class. She started by saying Da-Da—the initial sound of the first word in the sentence: Daddy. The children laughed and one boy, who had been left back in second grade, mocked her and said, "Da-Da Daddy!" The teacher chastised him immediately, but the harm was done. She chose to never read aloud again in class and, of course, her nickname from that day forward, including her high school years, became Da-Da.

But the joke wasn't entirely on her. She was a straight-A student and in eighth grade was named valedictorian of her graduating class. Her fascination with computers continued during her high school years where she became the "go-to" person for students and teachers. The IT specialists would ask for her help when they were having a particularly difficult time figuring out why their system was down or experiencing a problem.

No one was surprised when Tiffany was named valedictorian of her high school class and awarded a full scholarship to Princeton University for computer science. She had dreamed of becoming a computer engineer from the time she was in grammar school. Regarding her graduation, no one in the history of her school had ever attended Princeton on a full scholarship.

Attending Princeton was more than a culture shock; it was like being electrocuted. It was overwhelming! Interesting! Fascinating! Challenging! At the same time, it was a replay of earlier years. She didn't have the clothes like the other kids who seemed to have so much money. Everything she bought had to be put on a card that her mother paid for and, knowing how hard her mom worked, she bought very little. Other students spent time and money eating out; she always ate in her room—usually alone—after she purchased the food for her meal at a local grocery.

Never asked to join a sorority, she spent all of her free time working on her class assignments and thinking of new and interesting applications for computer software. She never missed a class or an assignment, and always chose to sit at the back of the class, a habit that started in grade school with the intent that if she was invisible, she would not be asked to read.

The four years flew by. In spite of her shyness, the professors recognized her talent and again, she was the class valedictorian, in spite of the withering competition.

Before graduation, she was contacted by three Silicon Valley corporate giants in the computer industry and offered seven-figure contracts, and signed up with one of them.

When Tiffany told her mom on the phone, her mom said, "Praise Jesus!" and began to weep uncontrollably. Her baby, the little girl she had thought about aborting, would become a millionaire.

During her time with the company, Tiffany met Sandra. Tiffany had never dated and was never attracted to any of the boys in high school or college. She didn't give it much thought. She was always too busy and had a difficult time with socialization. That is, until one Friday night while working late she met Sandra, who was very much like her. She also had a difficult time making friends; it was as if the universe conspired to bring them together: both brilliant, both wealthy, both with Asperger's syndrome, and now, as Tiffany realized, both gay.

Two years later, her mom was fired from her job, just two months before her retirement date. She called Tiffany and explained, through her sobs, that the company was moving to India and that she was no longer needed. She also told her that one of the upper management supervisors had pilfered the pension fund and the company was not taking responsibility for his actions. This meant that Mom would not be getting her pension and, though she might eventually win in court, it could take years. However, the company had no idea of the financial avalanche that would follow for messing with Tiffany's mom.

Tiffany told her Mom that she would always take care of her and not to worry. Being fiercely independent, Mom appreciated Tiffany's offer, but felt ashamed. Having to rely on charity was not part of her character; she was strong, independent, and now, very angry.

Tiffany went to work. The years of isolation and study had provided her with knowledge and insights into the arcane world of advanced computer science that was unmatched by anyone in her company. She decided that her mom would get her retirement pay, and furthermore, that she would send a message to corporations around the world who decided to take advantage of those who would not, or could not, fight back.

The following Monday, the chief financial officer of the company that fired mom called the CEO in a panic! Their account balance was zero!

Over the weekend, someone had hacked their system and transferred all their funds to locations around the globe. He had tried to identify the hacker as well as the accounts that received the money and was met with firewalls and computer wizardry that was beyond him. They contacted the FBI immediately and their experts encountered the same challenges. Whoever had hacked the system was a genius and only another genius could begin to understand the process.

Mom's company was the first of seven major corporations known for mistreating long-time employees by moving overseas and showing no consideration for the lives of men and women who had been loyal and hardworking. Panic followed! All of the companies had balance sheets with zero dollars.

Computer brainiacs around the world were consulted and no one was able to figure out how it had been done, who did it or where the money went. Furthermore, all seven of the hacked companies received an email on the same day from a source in Zululand, Africa. It advised the following:

1. Your funds will be returned when you make arrangements to begin the process of moving your company's headquarters from foreign soil back to the United States.
2. No more than ten percent of your facilities may be outside the continental United States.
3. All agreements between your employees concerning retirement, medical coverage, and other benefits will be honored.
4. All employees who have been terminated within five years of their pension due date will be rehired and allowed to complete their time in order to receive their promised benefits.

5. Failure to take action within one month of the date of this message will result in the transfer of your company's funds to organizations around the world to care for the poor.

The email was signed, *Daddy*.

The big boys and girls who captained the companies had taken out loans to get them by and were now running scared. The best were hired to figure it all out and always the same verdict: This is impossible!

After two weeks, another email arrived. This one was from Australia and stated:

> You are wasting your time! Do the right thing! You have two weeks left before the real pain begins. Daddy

There was more chaos. They decided to start to comply with the demands. As they did, money began to filter back to their accounts. The process took over a year and eventually all the money was returned and Tiffany's mom, as well as all the employees who had been terminated, received their full benefits without having to return to work.

During the year of transitions, repeated attempts to find the culprit(s) proved unsuccessful. Eventually, all of the demands had been met.

After one year to the day that the panic started, each of the hacked companies received a letter from the president of the company in the Silicon Valley that had been hired to help get their money back. It read:

Dear Sirs/Madams:

We apologize for not being able to assist in finding the offenders who caused your company near-financial ruin and certainly, much anxiety and grief.

We are delighted to hear that all of your fiscal resources have been returned and that your company is again enjoying financial success, as well as the good will of those employees who have been rehired.

Though we were not successful in completing the mission assigned us, I want you to know that my staff worked diligently and tirelessly in their efforts to assist you with this challenge.

Yours truly,
Tiffany Jones, President
Jones Consulting

CHAPTER 17

In Search of a Miracle

By Saturday, the ladies were all wondering what color tunic Kathleen would wear next. They seemed to think it would be purple, and they were right! The color contrast with her blond hair was complementary; she looked amazing! That night, instead of wearing a scarf, she wore a purple orchid over her left ear. However, since she entered from the left side of the stage, the ladies did not see the flower until she was in front of them. She asked, "Do you like the flower?" Their applause was enthusiastic. She said, "My colleague, the gentleman, who has been helping me develop and implement this seminar series, gave it to me. He raises orchids."

Kathleen began, "Tomorrow will be our seventh night together and the day you will complete your initiation ceremony. In all societies, as a boy becomes a man or a girl becomes a woman, there is an initiation ceremony. You are already women. However, none of you have had the experience of having your vibration elevated. I have invited very special guest to perform the ceremony. She will be introduced to you after my initial remarks and the presentation of your seventh story.

Many of the women turned to get the reaction of others in the group and it was obvious Kathleen's remarks had given them cause to reflect and wonder what she meant by this "change in vibration."

She sensed their concern and said, "Ladies, everything in this universe vibrates at a specific frequency. Even objects that seem to be solid are in fact vibrating. All of us vibrate because we are electrochemical magnets; some of us vibrate at a higher frequency and some at a lower frequency. Your vibration is your life energy. The higher your vibration, the more you are capable of doing and experiencing."

Her explanation seemed to satisfy the women for the moment, although the talk of the initiation process brought with it a group sense of heightened anxiety.

"I promise that your initiation is something you will enjoy and relive many times with fond memories. Its purpose is to bring you to a higher state of consciousness which will allow you to see and understand more of what is going on around you and also, give you the energy and insight needed to bring about change, where necessary. This change might be within you, your family, friends, co-workers, community or it might be on a larger scale, such as state, national or international venues.

The story you are going to read tonight is about a mother who fears for the life of her son; a mother with few resources who can't bare the pain of her son dying, or going to prison. She is a mom who tries in desperation to talk to her son, who hears only the call of vengeance in his heart. She is a mom in search of a miracle.

GERONIMO'S GOT A GUN!

by City Bear

Geronimo was far too immature to be walking around with a gun, but there was no convincing him otherwise. Small in stature and a poor student at PS 87 in the Bronx, the gun gave him a sense of power that he craved. He never felt he mattered. He was just a skinny black kid with an Native-American name and a dad he never knew. His Mom felt overwhelmed long before he was born and had a habit of talking to Jesus, as if he were in the room with her.

Mom had the courage of a lioness and her strength was based on her Christian faith. She wasn't afraid to express her thoughts to anyone, at any time, and whatever she thought had its roots in the Word of God, the Holy Bible. Still, she mused, *A person can take just so much! Lord have mercy, I can't take no more. Lord have mercy!* Mom's anguish had its roots in Geronimo's poor school work and attendance, as well as his choice of friends, and most of all, the gun!

Geronimo had been "jumped in," and at age thirteen was a full-fledged member of the Black Knights. He started carrying the day after his initiation beating and was proud of the fact that, even though one of his ribs was broken, he didn't cry. Every ounce of him wanted to cry, but he didn't. He wouldn't; he couldn't. He had turned the tear mechanism off long ago and replaced it with a rage that kept it securely in check. It was a rage that was fueled by fear; fear that he was a nothing—a skinny nothing, who would never read on grade level and be lucky to ever find a job. For Geronimo, none of that mattered now because, when he carried the gun, he had the power of life and death, and with that power, a sense of worthiness.

All of that changed the day Shorty was shot. His best friend since second grade, they did everything together. Shorty was a year older and was also a Black Knight. During Geronimo's jump in, Shorty pulled his kicks and punches so it looked like he was hurting his pal when, in fact, he wasn't. Geronimo loved Shorty like a brother. When he was killed by a rival gang, Geronimo's rage rose to fury and his only thoughts were about revenge.

Mom knew that Geronimo had a gun but he wouldn't tell her where he had it hidden. She knew her boy, and her motherly instinct told her that something had to be done before he avenged Shorty's death. She talked. She pleaded. She tried logic. When nothing worked, she resorted to what she knew best—prayer. Every morning and every night she prayed with the fervor of a prisoner seeking a governor's pardon from the death penalty.

No answer! She wondered, *Maybe the Lord doesn't want to hear me. I'm always asking for something and maybe, He's just tired of me. But Geronimo is my only boy and, if something happens to him, I won't want to live.* Mom knew she needed a miracle and was full of faith. She would often say, "You can't be a Bible woman, if you don't believe in miracles."

Geronimo had stopped going to school, and the truant officer had mom's number on speed dial. It didn't matter! Geronimo's time was spent being fully committed to the Knights and their talk, aside from girls, money, and drugs, focused on avenging Shorty. Whenever his name was mentioned, his tears screamed to be released, and he did all he could do to control himself. He coped with it by spitting out a stream of obscenities related to the killer and what was going to happen to him.

During one of Mom's prayer sessions, she was sent a message that she knew she had to follow. She was told, without words, to meet with her pastor and seek his counsel.

Pastor Williams was tall, thin, and drenched in the Word of God. He turned no one away and gave his time to all those who sought his guidance without judgment of their lifestyle, their sins or the sincerity of their repentance. He was the real deal—a true man of God—and anyone who paid attention could sense it.

When Pastor Williams opened the door, mom could no longer hold back the tears. She felt safe with him. Her tears were a mixture of sorrow and relief. She felt relieved knowing that she didn't have to bear her burdens alone, that someone cared, and that his interest and concern was sincere.

The pastor told her that he had just made some coffee and asked if she would join him. She did, and he brought her what looked like a fine china cup and saucer, as well as the milk, sugar and coffee pot. For the first few minutes she sipped at her coffee and composed herself. They sat in silence. When she seemed ready, he said, "Sister Simmons, I'd like to start with a prayer." They both bowed their heads and prayed:

> Dear merciful Lord, Sister Simmons needs your help and she needs it now. Please don't put her on the waiting list. She's been carrying a burden that brought her to me and my sense is that her and Job have a lot in common. Please guide me Lord and through your Holy Spirit, give me the wisdom to help this good woman in her time of need! I ask in Jesus's name. Amen.

Mom had no idea why but she felt a sense of peace; sense of relief, and yet, she hadn't told the pastor about why she was there.

"So, Sister Simmons, how may I be of service?"

"It's my boy, Pastor. He's with the Knights and you know what they up to and it never no good. His best friend, Shorty, be gunned down by the 79th Street Outlaws, and he got a gun and all he talk about is killin' that boy that shot Shorty. He don't go to school and the truant officer say that he pressin' charges, and Geronimo be charged and goin' to court. He only thirteen, so they ain't goin' do much and he know that. Pastor, I don't want my boy in jail for killin' that boy! I'm sick, Pastor. I work two jobs and it's so hard."

Pastor Williams took a sip of his coffee and looked in the cup as if the answer might be written on the bottom of it. He was silent and closed his eyes. Maybe a full minute passed before he answered. He said, "This Sunday, I'm giving a special service for mothers and I want you to sit in the front pew. I want to tell all the mothers about your son and I want all of us to pray together. That'll be a powerful prayer and I know the Lord will answer. Do I have your permission to share your story?"

Mom was too overwhelmed to speak. She had goose bumps from head to toe, and she nodded her head in agreement.

That Sunday, Pastor Williams invited Sister Simmons to stand with him as he told her story. He led them in prayer—a request that Geronimo be given the Divine Grace to change his life. There was silence. If a pin had been dropped on the marble floor, the congregation would have heard it. From the back of the church a woman began singing *Amazing Grace* with the voice of an angel. Pastor had never seen her before. She was a dark-skinned older woman, maybe in her eighties or possibly, nineties, with white hair and a huge white hat. She started softly and increased her volume as she progressed. The second time she sang the refrain, the entire congregation was singing with her and most of the women were crying. A sense of peace and calm had entered the church and the tears were not from sadness but rather, joy. Pastor had never witnessed anything like it.

After the service, Pastor Williams went to look for the woman with the white hat. She was gone! When he asked the ladies of the congregation if they had seen her, they all had the same response, "No Pastor!" often followed by a question like, "Where was she sitting?"

The following week, Geronimo was the same. There was no change! Then, he met Beverly Bostik at a local park. She was sitting on a bench and drawing a playground scene with kids laughing and running around. Her perspective was aerial, as if she were watching the scene from above.

When he passed by, Geronimo had been smoking weed with his friends. It was his only relief. After two weeks, the pain of losing Shorty was as deep and fresh as if it happened yesterday. It was late in the afternoon and Beverly knew Geronimo from class. They were both in the eighth grade.

"What you doin', Girl?" asked Geronimo.

Without looking up, she said, "What business of yours? Go smoke your weed with your loser friends."

The three Knights with him laughed, and Leroy said, "Ouch, G! That girl takin' a piece of you!"

Geronimo sat down next to Beverly and she said, "My Mom went to service last Sunday and they be prayin' for you. You goin' to jail, G, when you kill that boy. Geronimo didn't respond. He just sat there thinking that his mom's church people were praying for him. He had heard that the killer had fled to South Carolina, not fearing the police, but rather, the Knights, especially Geronimo.

Beverly closed her pad and said, "I got to go, G. I got choir practice in fifteen minutes. Why don't you come with me?"

Geronimo was not interested in the choir but he was interested in Beverly. She was different. She didn't curse or fool around with the boys. She was really smart and the teachers talked about her artwork. There was something about her, in addition maybe to the finest set of legs he had ever seen, made him want to follow.

Beverly told Sister Shirley, the choir director, that Geronimo was with her because he wanted to join the choir.

Geronimo looked like someone had hit him with a brick. Stunned! He was too stunned to answer and before he could think about it, he was standing next to Beverly holding a hymnal. At the choir director's lead, they began to sing hymn 197, *Amazing Grace.* Geronimo's voice was loud, clear, and exceptional.

An older woman in a white hat was seated in the front row listening to the choir. Everyone thought she was someone's grandmother.

She came and stood next to the director and motioned for the choir to let Geronimo continue by himself. And he sang, *Amazing Grace, how sweet thou art to save a wretch like me….*

It was beautiful—no, magnificent! Beverly and the other members were shocked. When he finished, the choir and the director applauded him. He had never felt that feeling before: loved, accepted, and competent. He also felt the presence of Shorty and realized that another killing wouldn't solve anything.

After practice, Sister Shirley went to look for the lady with the white hat but she had vanished. Geronimo had already left with Beverly, so she asked the remaining girls if anyone had seen the lady leave, and all responded with a variation of, "After Geronimo sang and we applauded, we didn't see her again! It was like she vanished!"

Shorty smiled down and thought, *Well done, G!*

CHAPTER 18

Expectations

Tonight's session started about five minutes late and the women were wondering if something was wrong. Kathleen had always been punctual and by the time she had arrived the murmering had become loud and the mood anxious. They applauded when she walked to the microphone and a sense of relief filled the air. They knew that tonight was the "big" night—the night of their initiation—although they were not sure exactly what that meant or what would be involved.

Kathleen wore a white tunic and once again, a purple orchid. She looked radiant with the contrast between the tunic, flower, blond hair, and a dazzling white smile. She smiled in recognition of their applause and said, "Sorry, I had a meeting earlier and the traffic getting back caused the delay! Please forgive me!"

By this time, the women loved her and pretty much whatever she did was just fine. A little tardiness didn't matter.

Kathleen began, "During the past week you have become a cohesive group and are no longer individuals who have just met each other. This is important and, as it was in the time of Sappho, when women come together with a common mission their power increases exponentially, as opposed to trying to do things by themselves. Our guest will not be arriving until 8 p.m. However, your story to be read later this evening before you go to bed is in the envelope at your place setting."

Kathleen outlined her expectations for the coming year and the women, who would be working together on a variety of projects, were divided into ten groups of seven. Each group was provided with instructions specific for their tasks and given the appropriate contact information needed to communicate. They were asked to consult each other at least weekly by whatever means they decided upon and to elect one member to keep notes that would be sent to the other members about each week's progress, as well as the activities to be initiated for the following week.

Time was set aside for questions and answers and, as the time approached 8 p.m., Kathleen reminded them to read their story for the night. Before she left the stage, she announced that their last time together would be at breakfast at 7 a.m. on Monday following which limousines would take them to the airport for their return home.

THE MAMA BEAR WHO SAVED HER CUBS AND CHANGED THE WORLD!

by City Bear

The old grizzly lumbered down the mountainside looking for something to eat. He was hungry and, being an omnivore, everything was on his menu. He hadn't found the quantity of fish that gave him the stores of fat needed to survive the winter. Instinctively, he knew he would die if he didn't put on the weight that would be lost during hibernation. It was now mid-October and soon the snow would be coming.

Nearby, the mama bear was tired and hungry. She had given birth to three cubs and their thirst for her milk seemed unquenchable. She had no idea that today her actions would echo around the world and bring about much needed change.

Without realizing it, the old grizzly and mama bear were on a collision course.

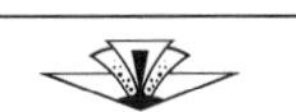

Jessie had tried for years to have a child but nothing seemed to work. One Sunday, totally distraught about not being able to conceive, she went to church, knelt before the statue of the Blessed Mother and asked, no, begged, for her to please help her to bear a child!

Jessie was thirty-seven and knew the time was coming when she would no longer be able to conceive. She thought about it every day. Although she had been successful in the eyes of the world as the marketing manager of a Fortune 500 advertising company, she still felt unfulfilled. She had attended more baby showers than she had wanted to remember, and at each one, a twinge of jealousy always accompanied the happiness she felt for the new mother. She coped by telling herself that she still had time, but recently, the positive thinking wasn't working. She was on the short side of desperate and she knew it.

For many years, she had been too busy on Sundays for church, attending to the things that during the week couldn't be addressed because her job started at eight in the morning and finished around eight at night.

Her husband, Dave, was a sweetheart. He never complained about the hours and, because he liked to cook, dinner was always prepared when she arrived home. He consoled her when she cried about not being able to have a child, and she loved him for that, as well as for the many kindnesses he showed her on a daily basis. Dave had been checked by his doctor, and according to the report, his sperm count was high enough to re-populate China!

Dave was a police detective in southern Manhattan and the most together man she had ever met. At five feet eight, she was two inches taller than him. If anyone had ever told her in her youth that she would marry a man shorter than she, she would have laughed at them. Then she met Dave.

The relationship began through a business connection. Her office had been broken into and computer equipment, as well as a cash box, had been stolen. Dave was the detective assigned to the case. When she first met him there was no magic. He seemed like a nice guy but he was all business. No flirting. He was professional and focused. He asked her questions and she answered. Two days later, he had caught the thief: a young mailroom employee with a heroin habit. She was especially grateful because he had stolen her personal computer on which there were important files and she had no copies.

Their second meeting was a little different. He explained how the thief had gained access after office hours and how he was able to remove half a dozen computers without being caught on camera, or noticed by the guard at the entrance to the building. The magic started during Dave's review of what happened and how. She thought, *There's something about this guy. He's not impressed with my position or how I look; he's together. No bragging, no swagger; just a guy doing a job which he's very good at.*

The meeting ended. The man had been arrested and was locked up awaiting a bail hearing. She thanked him and he left. There were no fireworks...but there was something.

Jessie went to lunch as usual with the company president, whom she called Mr. M. His real name was Muratore; an older man in his late eighties, he was more like a father than a boss. He was responsible for her being the marketing director and, over the years and with his continued support, she worked her way to the top. Today, Mr. M. had to go to the hospital to visit his sister, who was also in her late eighties and had recently fallen on her way home from church. When she arrived at the cafeteria, you would never believe who was waiting in line. You guessed it! Dave. *There are no coincidences!* She thought.

She asked, "Are you having lunch alone?" He responded, "Yes, unless some very attractive, mysterious woman invites me to join her." And he smiled and looked at her with his puppy-dog greenish-brown eyes. Her heart raced and she could feel her face flush. My God she thought, *I haven't reacted to a flirty line like that in years? What's going on?* In a tone intended to mask her feelings, she said, "I usually have lunch with the man who runs this place but he can't make it today. Would you like to join me?"

"Sure." he responded.

They sat together and talked first about the case and then about places and things they both enjoyed including Greenwich Village, the Guggenheim Museum, their favorite Broadway plays, and the New York Giants. The first time she looked at her watch, she realized she was half an hour late for an office appointment. Jessie said, "Oh Boy! I was having so much fun, I forgot about the time. I need to get back." He stood up when she went to leave and shook her hand. That was it. He shook her hand and smiled. He never said goodbye, nice to meet you, blah, blah, blah!

Jessie's afternoon was uneventful. However, there was something else. It was his scent: Bay Rum. Her father had always used Bay-Rum, an after shave that's been around forever. She wondered if that was part of the attraction and she also wondered if she'd ever see him again.

The following day at about 9:00 a.m., her secretary called and told her that a detective from a downtown Manhattan precinct was waiting outside and had some additional items that had been recovered. She responded, "Please ask him to wait, I'll be just a minute." Her pulse quickened, she took out her pocket mirror and checked her hair and makeup. She took a deep breath and did her best to act insouciant before calling back the secretary to send him in.

Disappointment! Dave had sent his partner, Ralph, to bring back the cash box and some other items that had been recovered. Ralph was a little over six feet, with an olive complexion and black, slicked-back hair. His suit was beautifully tailored and his Italian loafers looked new. When he explained how the additional loot was found, she didn't hear a word he said. Her thoughts were about Dave. When she caught herself, she thought, *I'm acting like a sophomore school girl.* She laughed.

Ralph said, "Did I say something funny?" Embarrassed, Jessie said, "I'm sorry, I'm just thinking of something amusing that happened this morning." Meeting over and Jessie went back to work.

The following day, during lunch with the boss, she caught herself drifting to the conversation with Dave. She was preoccupied when Mr. Muratore asked, "Is there something wrong? You don't seem like your usual self today." Jessie responded, "I stayed up last night watching *The African Queen* for the tenth time." He responded, "Bogart was really special. I've been a big fan of his forever!" Some additional chitchat and they both went back to their offices.

When Jessie got back to her desk, she continued to ruminate; *I wonder if I'll ever see him again?* Immediately thereafter, the secretary rang and said, "There's a detective here to see you. Heart pounding, she hoped it was Dave and not his partner. She responded, "Just a moment. Tell him I'll be with him shortly!"

Again, she went through the routine of the mirror, the hair, the deep breath, and the air of indifference. She phoned the secretary to send him in and Mr. Wonderful entered. Jessie was a clean nut and that morning it had rained. At the entrance to her office, she had placed a black rubber mat that folks could wipe their feet on. As Dave walked in, he tripped on it and began falling onto the floor. It was amazing! Once he knew he was falling, he rolled and came back up on his feet.

"How did you do that?" Jessie asked.

"Nineteen years of Aikido. It's second nature. I don't have to think about it."

"Good to see you, Dave. I enjoyed our lunch conversation and hope I didn't keep you away from your work for too long."

He responded, "That's why I'm here. I haven't enjoyed myself like that in years. I'm divorced. My wife went for some minor nip and tuck. I didn't think she needed it and ended up falling in love with the plastic surgeon.

We didn't have any children, so it was bad, but it could have been a lot worse. That's why I'm here!"

Jessie responded, "Because your wife ran away with her doctor?" They both laughed. Dave said, "No, because, I'd like to have you for dinner. I mean, I'd like to have dinner with you." They laughed again; this time a little louder. This is getting interesting, she thought.

Dave continued, "I'm divorced almost five years and you're the first woman that's really interested me. I know that probably sounds like a pick-up line, but I mean it. Look, I'm a cop and I don't make anywhere near the money you make, but it's just dinner. I want to continue the conversation."

Jessie thought, *We're both liars, we say we want to continue the conversation but what we really want has nothing to do with words!*

A year and many conversations later they were married. After ten years into a marriage that romantics write stories about, she couldn't conceive. After getting up from bed one morning, a month after Jessie's plea to the Blessed Mother, she felt sick to her stomach. Wow! That was quick she thought. Her devotion would continue for the rest of her life.

The draft has been reinstated and the little boy that she adored was now twenty-years old. She remembered combing his hair before school and making sure that his clothes were clean, pressed, and the latest fashion. She spoiled him rotten and Dave took care of the discipline—although not much of that was needed because Patrick was a really good kid.

She knew what the letter was when it arrived in the mail. Marked "U.S. Government," it was his official draft notice. *My God,* she thought. *I don't want him to go.* Patrick wanted to be a surgeon. All his life from the time he was a little boy, he spoke of being a doctor and later, a surgeon: a pediatric surgeon. He loved kids and wanted to help children who needed miracles. He wanted to create miracles with his hands.

Jessie was beside herself and did not want her beautiful, talented Patrick to go into the army to become cannon fodder. Her company made commercials for the armed services and she knew exactly what the marines were doing when they said, "We need a few good men" and the army, when they told young people, "You can be an army of One!" She knew it was all bullshit and directed at young men, and more recently young women, who for a variety of reasons, had limited educational or vocational options and wanted to feel respected and admired by their family and friends. Usually, at least for the young men, the commercials were created in recognition of their overabundance of testosterone—the hormone that made them race motorcycles, drink too much, and think every fifteen seconds about sex. By age twenty-five, even the most pumped up on testosterone know better than to think he can be an army of one!

Jessie wept! The thought of her son in a foreign land fighting a war that probably wouldn't be won, both scared her and, at the same time, made her angry. The date was approaching for Patrick's induction and Dave said, "There's nothing you can do. If he doesn't go, they'll put him in jail." They had a month before Patrick would leave.

By this time, Dave had made Captain and Jessie was busier than ever. The draft notice had them totally stressed and, in recognition of their emotional overload, Dave said, "Jess, let's go away on a vacation. We need one. We need to get away."

It was the end of September when they decided to go to Yellowstone. They arrived on the 13th of October and Jessie had no idea how this trip would define the rest of her life.

Most of the tourists had headed home, except for the retirees who had all the time in the world to camp and tour. They stayed at one of the best hotels in the park. The views were breath-taking and the smells of the forest and fields made them wonder how they had survived living in New York for so long. They felt more alive than they had in years and somewhere, someone was burning leaves. That wonderful smell brought back childhood memories for both Dave and Jessie.

They were both early risers and had signed on for a guided tour of a remote area in the Western region of the park. Mountains, rivers, geysers, forests, and fields—Yellowstone had it all. Their breakfast had been a gourmet's dream and they had forgotten about the ominous induction date.

In a conversation with Dave before their trip, Jessie said, "During the First and Second World Wars we had to fight. There was no choice or we would now be speaking German or Japanese; but these last wars? Vietnam was an atrocity. All those beautiful young men and women killed, and for what? What did we accomplish?" Dave just listened.

She continued, "The Russians lost in Afghanistan. What makes us think we can win and what exactly is it we'll win? Nineteen Saudi men flew into the World Trade Center and killed thousands. What did we do? We invaded Iraq, while a former president held hands with the Saudi King. It's all bullshit Dave! All smoke and mirrors, and the American people don't know any better because they are lied to by the news media. Americans are good people, but they have been sold a bill of goods because in war lots of people make obscene amounts of money. What makes it worse is that now the government wants to take God out of everything.

Jessie continued, "And what really makes me angry is the men and women who are killed or wounded. They, and their families, are not properly cared for. The VA is a corrupt mess and we shouldn't need the Wounded Warrior Project, which I have great admiration for, to care for our returning vets. Our government gives billions to countries that hate us and we don't take care of the men and women who bravely served and now, need our help. It's bullshit Dave."

Dave thought, *She only says bullshit when she is over the top furious!*

Jessie's company had been involved for many years in developing and implementing commercials used by the armed services to entice young men and women to join. More than once, she had heard the commercial creators laughing in the cafeteria about how easy it was to play on the needs for acceptance and recognition of those whose frontal lobes had not fully developed. The frontal lobe of the brain for men is not fully developed until about the age of twenty-five. Its function has to do with critical thinking and decision making.

After being married to Jessie for twenty-one years, Dave knew not to interrupt. She was on a roll and eventually the diatribe would end. She kept rolling.

"Dave, what really makes me nuts is that no one does anything about it. Many people know what I know and all they do is gripe. I can't think of a mom or dad who wants their son or daughter to go to war unless there's a really good reason, like we're being invaded! These last conflicts aren't even called wars and none of them have been approved by Congress."

Still silent, after she finished, Dave took her hand, kissed it, and said, "I'm worried about Patrick." She responded, "I am an emotional and physical wreck. I don't know what to do. He's my life, Dave!"

The jeep was about to leave and they climbed in. Their companions included an elderly couple from Alberta, Canada, and three young guys in their late teens or early twenties. The guide was a woman who was about thirty, and who also worked as a smoke jumper for the forestry department.

At first, they looked like four small dots coming down the mountain. As the group got closer, they thought they were dogs and, as the distance closed, it was unmistakable…a mother and three bear cubs. About a quarter of a mile above and to the left of the bears appeared another dot. This one, however, was bigger and, as he closed on the mama bear and cubs, he was almost twice her size. She saw him coming about a hundred yards away. She had sniffed the air and turned to see him charging.

"Oh, my God, Dave! That huge bear is going to kill the cubs. Maybe he'll kill all of them! We have to do something."

The guide overheard Jessie and said, "Sometimes what happens is not what you think will happen!"

Mama bear stood up and raced at the bigger male like a fearless, undersized line-backer going to drop a big fullback. They collided and mama bear was pushed back but her attack was ferocious. She bit and clawed for all she was worth and was bleeding from her right shoulder. She had clawed his face and he roared in answer. Both were wounded, and then the most interesting thing happened, he turned and walked away. Mama bear and her cubs would survive, as long as she didn't die from her wound.

Dave had been captivated. He turned to Jessie and said, "Holy shit Jess! Did you see that?"

Of course she had seen it and her response was quite different. She said, "Dave, I know how we're going to handle Patrick's induction."

"What does that have to do with the bear fight?"

"You'll see, Dave!" She wouldn't talk about it for the rest of the trip.

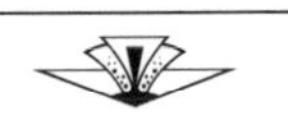

When she returned to her job, Jessie requested a meeting with Mr. Muratore. He had lost his only son in Vietnam and his mourning never ended. They say time heals all wounds; not so for the boss. He visited Arlington cemetery three or four times a year and cried his eyes out for a son who had just begun his adult life. Despite his age, Mr. Muratore took great pride in his physical appearance, and at six feet one, he could still fit into his U.S. Marine uniform. He had been a member of the great Pacific theater battles. He was still proud to have served. However, he would never speak about the war. He was also very unhappy about the direction of our country, especially about getting involved in questionable conflicts that never seemed to solve anything.

She was his first meeting of the day and they both had cups of coffee. She told him about Patrick and her concerns. He understood better than most because he lost his son. She told him about the bear encounter and how it had changed her. She told him that she would be willing to die rather than have Patrick go to a war that wasn't even a declared war, and had no chance of winning for purposes that, at best, seemed vague.

"What do you have in mind?" he asked.

"We've made commercials for the armed services to get young men and women to join. Now I want to make a commercial that will keep them out!"

"I don't get it?" he responded.

"We are going to make a commercial and I'm asking, not just American moms, but all the mothers of the world: the Afghans, the Iranians, the Iraqis, and the Syrians, all of them. I'm asking all mothers to join with me to tell their governments that war is over. When they come to get my son, I will be armed and I will shoot whoever comes to take him, knowing that I will probably die. And Patrick will make a video recording the confrontation and make it go viral by sending it to hundreds of his friends, who will send it to hundreds of their friends, and so on."

When she got home she told Dave, who had nothing to say in return. Later that evening, he came into the bedroom with glasses of

Chardonnay for them both. He said, "I've had a good life, Babe. If you decide to do this, you're not going to do it alone."

Next, she told Patrick about her plan. He said, "Mom, no! Please no! They'll end up killing all of us."

She responded, "Patrick, your Dad and I have made plans for you to go to Canada. Many people in your same situation went there in the sixties and lived good lives."

"Mom, you can't do this! I'd rather die than see something happen to you and Dad."

Jessie couldn't be persuaded to change her mind. Patrick agreed to set up the video and make the connections to YouTube, Facebook, Twitter and over two hundred blog sites around the world. After many heated family arguments that left everyone in tears, Patrick agreed to go to Canada.

They were warned what would happen when they came to get Patrick. Patrick had already left for Canada but returned home the night before he knew they'd be coming for him. Dave and Jessie couldn't convince him to leave. Mr. Muratore knew when it was all going down and, on the day of reckoning, rang the doorbell at 7:00 a.m. wearing his meticulously appointed U.S. Marine uniform.

The U.S. Marshals did not expect what was waiting for them. Most folks would expect that representatives from the U.S Army do the conscription; however, not so, it's the Marshals.

Dave and Jessie were armed with hunting rifles, as was Mr. Muratore, when the Marshal rang the doorbell, Dave told him that they were all armed and were ready to start shooting if anyone tried to take Patrick. Immediately, he called his supervisor and reinforcements followed in about an hour.

Patrick had it on camera and was ready to send out the video to the world.

The Marshal in charge commanded with a bullhorn that Patrick be sent out. He stated that no one would be hurt if they obeyed his orders.

Dave went to the door unarmed and called to speak with him. He told him about the video, the cameras, the blogs, and how everything would go viral.

The Marshal went back to his car and called his supervisor. The word that came back was for them to take the young man. To do what was necessary!

A few minutes later and just before all hell was about to break loose, the Marshal received another call from his boss. He said, "Stand down. Stand down."

The fearless mama bear's action had changed the world.

CHAPTER 19

The Visitor

After Kathleen left the stage, the lights dimmed and the women became silent as they waited for whatever was to happen next.

At exactly 8.00 p.m., the chimes of the temple bells signified the arrival. Three distinct chimes echoed through the hall, the lighting continued to diminish until the room became dark. Immediately thereafter, a pinpoint of light appeared on the ceiling in front of the stage. As it traveled downward, it widened and finally, opened to become a circle, in the middle of which stood a tiny woman, maybe four feet tall, whose robe glowed like white phosphorescence.

The response was an immediate "Oh!" and the women were focused with laser attention on the apparition. It seemed as if everyone in the room had stopped breathing and were holding their breath in anticipation of what would happen next.

In a tone and cadence that we might associate with someone with a hearing impairment, a little flat and more measured than we're used to, she announced:

> "I am Miriam and I come to you from the star system you know as the Pleiades. You call them the seven sisters. I arrived here long ago on a starship hidden from sight beneath your Atlantic Ocean near the island you know as Bimini. I am here to help you save your world before it is too late and it is very close to becoming too late.

The women were in awe! They expected a surprise, maybe

Richard Gere, George Clooney or the Dalai Lama, but this was nothing like them. Miriam's appearance and monologue would forever change the way the people of the world looked at their history, as well as their future. At that moment, every woman saw the insignificance of most things in their lives. Except for their families, the only thing that mattered was learning what they could do to bring about the needed change. It was the 911 of metaphysics.

> You have been lied to by your governments, as well as the media which, as you know, is controlled by a few wealthy men. They think of you as puppets who can be lulled to sleep and indifference with games, gadgets, and worthless paper which has become the prize that motivates most of your societies. This paper upon which ink displays pictures and numbers has become exalted to the point of worship. As an outsider, it is very clear, and by the end of this evening's activities, you will see your world far differently than you do now. I am here to begin the process of lifting the veils of your misunderstanding!

The silence continued. It was overwhelming. She paused for about fifteen seconds before speaking again:

> The reason each of you has been chosen is because of your concern for others. You see, everything in your universe and across all universes is vibrating. Your physicists know this, as do many others who have an interest in such things. Your entrance fee for this adventure was the commission of a random act of kindness. Many women in your world appear to be something they are not. They may seem to be kind and considerate toward others; however, when asked to do something for someone who can do nothing for them in return, many choose to ignore the supplicant, though they have far more than they need. Congratulations, for passing the first test!

The silence was accompanied by an almost complete lack of movement, as if the women were frozen in their seats. Again, Miriam hesitated, this time it was longer, maybe twenty seconds, before she spoke.

> Each of you will now have to make a choice. You may leave, if you feel that what I am asking you to do in helping me bring about major, much needed change in your world is something that you will not, or currently, cannot, do. Before you decide, I want to tell you that by the end of this evening you will not be the same woman who entered this room. Those of you who decide to stay will be initiated by me and given powers currently unavailable to you. So, if you think accomplishing the mission may be beyond you, you are right! That will change after your initiation. Those for whom this task seems too great, I invite you to return to your room.

Miriam waited. No one was leaving. Thirty or more seconds passed before she continued. She opened the inside of her robe and took out what appeared to be a sword, but unlike any sword known to humankind. It seemed to be made of a shimmering, white light. She raised it above her head, as if she were holding a torch, and as she did so, in an instant, she was standing on the floor level with the women and beside her was a little girl holding a wooden box.

> I am here to announce the return of the sacred feminine power. For far too long your world has been ruled by men without the balance of the sacred feminine. In all universes, as in your own, balance is essential for the survival of life. When there is too much male or female energy, there is a lack of balance. This lack of balance becomes exaggerated as the amount of male or female energy increases beyond the tipping point. When this happens, the energy in depletion must be increased and the energy in the majority decreased until balance is restored.

Miriam paused.

The return of the sacred feminine does not mean the Sacred Masculine is negative, or not needed, but rather, that for your world to survive, balance must be restored and that your worship of paper be understood for what it is: an illusion. It only has meaning because you give it meaning. A thousand years ago, if you had tried to buy something with this paper that you call money, you would have been laughed at. It had no meaning because the people did not agree that it had meaning. They had different kinds of money that was usually made of some metal that had an agreed-upon value.

There was some movement in the audience. The talk about money had been unsettling and the concept of illusion was still percolating in their minds.

Since you have decided to stay, I am going to explain what will be happening in the next few minutes. The object you watched me take from my robe is the Sword of Enlightenment and, as its name implies, it brings light to the darkness of misunderstanding or ignorance. It will also bring with it a charge of higher energy that will be felt throughout your body as you are touched by it. In essence, as I touch each of you on your right and left shoulder, a current of energy will pass into your body that will change the frequency of your vibration to a higher level of consciousness. Following this, you will never be able to return to your old self and your current consciousness."

The movement in the audience increased, as did the anxiety. Miriam paused and let the tension express itself.

One of the ladies raised her hand and after being acknowledged asked, "Suppose I don't like the new and improved me? My life is not so bad. I kind of like it. I'm not sure I want to do this!"

Miriam responded, "Please consider the following questions: Are you worried about the future of your children? Do you feel they have been given a world that provides them the opportunities that you had as a child? Do you feel that man's hatred for other men, often based on religious intolerance, can bring your children a world of peace and mutual co-existence or, are you concerned that one day you will wake up and the world, as you knew it, will no longer exist? Do you believe that the direction in which your world is moving will eventually bring about health, happiness, and fulfillment or, war, poverty and eventual annihilation?"

About halfway through Miriam's discourse, the woman started nodding her head in agreement so that by the time Miriam had finished, it was obvious she was committed. There were no further questions and so Miriam walked toward the first table of women. She asked all to remain seated except for the woman to be initiated.

Miriam gestured for the first initiate to stand. The woman gave a fake smile that, for many of us, signifies apprehension, as though she was about to jump out of an airplane for the first time or embark on a zip line experience.

Miriam touched the sword to her left shoulder and then, raising it over her head, touched her right shoulder. Once her right shoulder had been touched, the sound began: a low-pitched hum that seemed to come from the floor. It felt as if the floor was vibrating with the sound. Then, the little girl handed the initiate a candle from the box and when the transfer was made, the candle lit, as if by magic. It was a moment in time the women would never forget.

Miriam made her way from table to table and, after each anointing, the girl gave the woman a candle that spontaneously ignited as the sound of the hum increased in volume and depth. By the time Miriam had touched the shoulders of the last woman, the room was literally vibrating until finally, it was done! Each woman had received the touch of Miriam's sword.

Miriam raised the sword above her head and instantly, she and the little girl were back at center stage. The hum and vibrating floor ceased.

Visibly, the women looked the same as they had before the initiation with the exception that they seemed more awake and relaxed:

as if the energy enhancing process was accompanied by a deep state of relaxation.

Miriam placed the sword back inside her robe and when she began to speak, the little girl vanished.

> "Each of you has received a candle. It is to remind you that the most overpowering darkness can be easily overcome by one single light. Darkness prevails only when good people refuse to show their light. When you received your candle it was to remind you that you are now in the light—enlightened. Your vibration has changed and now you realize that your time on Earth, even if it seems very long, is actually very short. You understand that what really matters is kindness and that there is not enough time to do all the good things that need to be done. If you feel apprehensive, it is good. It means you realize the importance of what you have to do."

Julia, a stunningly beautiful, raven-haired woman in her forties, who now looked like she was in her thirties, thought, *I can never tell my family my vibration was raised by a woman who looked like Tinkerbell in a prom dress who carried a Star Wars sword of light and came to Earth from a Mothership. They'd ask, "Mom, are you eating too many organic veggies?" Or maybe, "Mom, are you sure the mushrooms you had for dinner are FDA certified?"*

As she continued, Miriam's voice had an edge to it that had not been heard before. She said, "It is very important that you tell no one about what happened tonight. I tell you this because many will not believe you and you will have to spend time and energy defending yourself. You will need both to complete your mission."

She repeated herself in a tone even more severe than previously, and said, "You must not tell what happened tonight to anyone; even your closest friends and family."

There was something almost threatening in her voice and, as the anxiety level in the room went from placid to panic, the hum returned and the floor vibrated. At the same time, the women felt an immediate sense of calm and, as they focused on Miriam, her voice became firm and commanding, like a general who was preparing the troops for the fight of their lives:

> Your mission, ladies, is to change the power structure of the United States. You will do so by running for the U.S. House of Representatives and the U.S. Senate. Most of the politicians do not care about you and their behavior has demonstrated their disregard for everyone but themselves. They make laws that you must follow but they do not. The lobbyists, who control their votes, will learn when you are in office that there are new sheriffs in town who cannot be bought or sold.
>
> It's not just the government that must be changed, there are other systems that must be challenged and amended: education, family, religion, corporations, communication, along with our attitudes toward Mother Earth, climate, poverty, health, and peace. I am especially concerned that families come together and realize the importance of their old and their young. All have a purpose and all are deserving of love and respect.
>
> While this may sound odd from someone like me, I'm asking each of you to pray morning, noon and night to the Creator of all that is and ever will be or, the deity you recognize to guide, bless, protect and heal or world. Your prayer should be simple: Name the deity of your choice and ask that Mother Earth, and all who dwell upon her, be guided, blessed, protected and healed, as it should be now and forever.
>
> Finally, for those who are non-believers, you may remind yourself throughout the day to let your light within shine allowing others to see the goodness within you. Think of your prayers and requests as rays of light firing like rockets from the Earth into infinity.

Her voice then returned to normal when she said:

> All of you will be contacted in the next few weeks and you will be given the financial assistance and guidance you need to make the mission a success. Based on your interests and abilities, each of you will be notified about the area of concern that has been chosen for you to address. You are not on your own, you now have a family, in addition to your current family, that will support your efforts and be with you for the rest of your life. You must succeed! As integrity returns to the United States, eventually, the rest of the world will follow.

When she had finished speaking, the light of each hand-held candle mysteriously extinguished. Only the spotlight surrounding Miriam was visible, but gradually it became smaller and smaller until it became a pinpoint on the ceiling above the stage. The house lights were turned on and Miriam was gone!

CHAPTER 20

Purple Politics

Breakfast had been served and the dishes removed from the tables when Kathleen addressed the group. Today, she wore a blue business suit, which made her look very corporate: matching shoes and scarf with a string of pearls. This was the first time the women had seen her in something other than a tunic.

She smiled and addressed them.

"Today you graduate. Today you go back to the real world and begin making those changes that you have identified as being your mission. I have discussed this with all of you individually in our sessions and it is now up to you to move forward at the speed and direction which challenges you. Please remember, if you are not challenging your comfort zone, you are not growing.

"Before I introduce my guest, I would like to review briefly the stories you have read this past week; each were designed to evoke a specific awareness.

"*The Power of Forgiveness* provided two examples of how life can change in a heartbeat when we are fully informed of the big picture. While letting go of anger can be very difficult for many of us, the path to emotional freedom and joy will never be found until we learn to forgive others, and most of all, ourselves.

"*Just a Fourth Grade Teacher* provided the example of a woman who was called to bring about changes in the Catholic Church and whose example can have a world-wide influence on the health and happiness of millions of people. Use it to identify your calling.

"*The Cruelest Joke* was a story about a mother's desire to bring about justice for her daughter by thinking "outside the box" and orchestrating a situation to do so. How might you think outside the box to remedy a difficult family situation?

"*Erin the Terrible* focused on the exploits of a young woman who refused to be beaten by the power of big corporations and thereby reinvented herself. Is there something you can do, in a large or small way, to harness your power to bring about change?

"*Da-Da Jones*, in some ways similar to *Erin the Terrible*, addressed the wrongs done to many folks who work for companies that mistreat their employees. This story suggested that humble beginnings, given the right talent and circumstances, can have world-altering endings. Do not limit your potential to make a difference.

"*Geronimo's Got a Gun!* was written for every mother who has a child whose problems seem insurmountable. This story reminded us that that we are not alone and that the power of prayer to bring about angelic or divine intervention is available to anyone who asks. The power of prayer can move mountains!

"The final story, *Mama Bear* revealed the potential of one woman to bring about peace. The heroine's actions demonstrate that, as a mother bear will die protecting her cubs, she was willing to give her life to change a system that provides untold riches for old men who finance and perpetrate wars that young men fight.

"As you leave today, your mission begins. You will not be on your own, but rather, each of you will continue to be coached by myself and my colleague. Because I have come to know each of you on a level deeper, in many ways, than your best friend or family members, our work together will be both challenging and personally rewarding.

"Each week, you will receive an email outlining what is expected of you. You will respond by providing me with your thoughts, worries or questions. We are in this together and you will never be asked to do something beyond your capacity. Working together, we will make good things happen!

"And now for your first gift!"

Similar to the flower Kathleen had worn the night before, each of the women was given a purple orchid set in a small, white ceramic pot filled with dirt. There was also an envelope attached to the pot that contained directions for the care of the flower.

"Sisters, the Purple Orchid Society will champion women who want to enter politics in the United States on a local, state, and federal level. Every woman we endorse will be vetted to ensure that they are the person for the job. We will not sponsor someone just because they are female. That would be a mistake! We will look at each woman's track record and determine if she has those qualities we believe are prerequisite for successful service—qualities such as: honesty, sincerity, integrity, and an ability to get the job done must be present for her to receive our support.

For those who do not enter the world of politics, the changes you make within yourself, your family, community, place of worship and workplace will serve as examples of change that will be heartening and desired by others.

"As most of you know, there are more women in the United States than men and, if we work together, we can become a powerful voice in what is currently male-dominated politics. This does not mean we want to have an all-female House and Senate, but rather, to work toward a balance of male and female representatives.

"And now the guest I promised."

With her introduction, a man walked on to the stage wearing a deerskin, waist-length jacket, dungarees with a large, silver belt buckle, a denim shirt and light-brown cowboy boots. Many of the women looked perplexed. He looked familiar, but most couldn't place him.

"I'd like to introduce you to the man who wrote the stories given to you. All of you interacted with him because he served as your bellman and brought your luggage to your room. He also assisted you during the week with scheduling appointments and providing transportation services. His name tag read: CB, whom you now know as City Bear.

"No doubt, you recall that during our first meeting I announced that my name is Kathleen, but that my name doesn't matter. What I meant was my name doesn't tell you who I am; it doesn't tell you about my spirit. City Bear was given his name by the man we were asked to call Coach—a man thought by many to be a legend or a myth. Both City Bear and I have been instructed and initiated by him after spending a week on his ranch in Arizona. Throughout the world, he is known as the Gifted One—a name given to him by the abbot of his monastery where his gift for healing was first recognized. Coach calls these spirit names, Indian names, and the name he gave me was Angel Heart. Of course, I was very flattered."

Kathleen looked at City Bear as his cue to begin.

"Ladies, I was the first initiate and Kathleen followed me. Our Coach had been invited by the abbot of his monastery to come to the United States to train three people who will begin the process of bringing about needed changes in our world. In order to do so, many of our systems will have to be challenged and restructured. This will take time, skill, perseverance, and an attitude that will not accept failure. We will be working toward creating a tipping point at which time these changes will be accepted. In many ways, the future of our children and grandchildren will depend on your success."

The women were doing their best to follow what was going on: the Coach, the training, the initiations, the Indian names, and the expectations. It was more than a little overwhelming.

City Bear continued, "By serving as your bellman, I was able to learn how each of you treated someone who could be perceived as your servant. Theophane was correct in choosing every woman here because all of you treated me with kindness and dignity. In getting to know you, I was able to assist Kathleen in determining your spirit name. We hope you find our analysis on target. The name we have chosen for each of you will be announced to you as both Kathleen and I thank you for your time and service when leaving this room."

It was Kathleen's cue to continue.

"Sisters, the purple orchid each of you has received is to remind you to take care of yourself as you take care of this beautiful flower. As the orchid needs sunlight, the right amount of water and proper climate, you need non-GMO food, pure water, exercise, relaxation, meaningful work, a relationship with the Creator and someone or something to love. Tonight, it is our intention to provide you with the knowledge, skill and ability to make a difference in your world, which is also our world. Care for your orchid and care for yourself and your loved ones. We will also be establishing a website where you can share your trials, tribulations and successes with your Purple Orchid sisters.

"Again, all of you will be contacted on a weekly basis as we work together to achieve your goals for our planet and everything that lives on it."

None of the women were in a great rush to leave. City Bear and Kathleen waited at the door. They went table by table and with their parting words and hugs, every woman was given her spirit name. A woman from China smiled at her name, "Humble Dragon." A woman from New York laughed when she heard, "Walks with a Purpose" and a very opinionated woman from Italy nodded her head in agreement after hearing, "Mama My Way."

By the time the room was empty, every woman had been given a spirit name and every woman carried with her their remembrance: a purple orchid in a white ceramic pot.

Their journey had begun!

CHAPTER 21

Lunch at the Grande Bretagne

The activities of the morning over and Kathleen and City Bear felt both energized and overwhelmed. Speaking with seventy people and expressing parting pleasantries had taken its toll. They were both now experiencing the high that precedes the crash, and they knew it.

CB said, "We've been here a week but have never had an opportunity just to sit and talk. Would you have time for lunch before you leave?"

"Sure," she answered.

They walked to the bar area and seated themselves far enough away from the noise of the crowd so they could talk without having to strain to hear each other.

Kathleen asked, "Your impression of the week?"

CB laughed, "Which part?"

"The whole thing!" she responded.

CB thought about it, "Well, let's see…Coach tells me to come to this hotel and act as the bellman. He sets it up with the hotel manager so that I get to welcome every woman and effectively be their servant for the week. You and I have never really had a chance to talk until now because you have to spend an hour with each woman, as well as prepare for your evening program, and I'm thinking I should have brought roller skates to get around faster.

"Fortunately, Boston Lou, one of the Coach's assistants, made sure I completed the stories before arriving because I could never have done anything creative during this past week. When we have more time, I'll tell you about Lou. For now, I'll just say that we have become close friends and he now lives in a furnished room over my garage."

Kathleen was happy to have someone else do the talking and listened without interruption.

"Because I'm the friendly type, three of the women invited me to their room to fix small things that didn't really need fixing: a drape that wouldn't close; a TV remote that didn't work, and things like that! Then, when I'd get to their rooms, they'd be wearing enticing lingerie—more than enticing; these outfits could set off fire alarms! And more than once, they would make *double entendres* that at any other time would have ended with me spending the night.

"After each temptation, I thought, *This would never happen if I wanted it to. It's always at a time when the fantasy can't become a reality.*"

Kathleen listened with an amused smile.

"Okay! My thoughts about the week! The hotel is magnificent and, without question, world class. The women were charming, sincere, and not spoiled. Even those who are very wealthy and used to getting their way never pressured me or spoke to me in a condescending manner. It was interesting but, at the same time, exhausting."

CB seemed as if he had more to say but needed to compose his thoughts. The brief silence gave Kathleen an opportunity to interrupt politely.

"Star spoke about you every day when I was at the ranch," she said. "You were definitely on her mind and, when she did, I always got the impression that you two might have a future together."

CB made a slight grimace that suggested concern.

"Is there a problem," she queried.

"She's returning to her husband, who has a drinking problem and told her that if she didn't come back, he'd kill himself."

"Wow! I'll bet that was a curve ball you never saw coming."

"Yeah, and I think it might be strike three for me and my relationship with her. I wish I didn't feel this way, but this is one of those things that just happens. You can't plan it. I feel like a teenager when the girl he wants to take to the prom has told him that she already has a date. I can really relate to Barney Fife on the old *Andy Griffith Show* when his girlfriend goes to the movies with Goober on a Thursday night when they have always gone to the movies on Thursday. When he tells Andy, he smiles this little self-contained smile and says, 'Yah, Andy, lots of fish in the sea, lots of shells on the beach,' and then proceeds to have a meltdown. That's me; I'm Barney. And I'm half way saying that I need a hug but I'm not going to because real men never say they need a hug! At least, I don't think they do!"

They both laughed and it felt good.

What about you? What are your thoughts of the week?"

Kathleen smiled, "The glasses were amazing. I felt like I had superpowers, and in a way, I did. I knew what the women were thinking and what they were attempting to hide. I was cautious in my approach with each of them and never made any of them feel ashamed or guilty for a wide variety of what might be considered poor judgments and actions motivated by jealousy, anger, lust, greed or pride. I helped them to accept the reality that we are all a combination of good and not so good. It's the human condition. But you'd be surprised at how many people torture themselves daily for things long past."

CB was intrigued by what Kathleen had to say and thought that many of these meetings must have been gut-wrenching.

"I tried to make it clear to all that we can't love someone else until we love ourselves first. Many had a problem with this. They were so used to giving to others and putting themselves last that they would eventually burn out.

"Many, too, could not forgive themselves for actions they had taken earlier in their lives. Most often, it had to do with the termination of pregnancies. While some women had no problem with this decision, others had difficulty in forgiving themselves. In order for them to be effective in their mission, I explained that everyone wishes they could revisit some of life's decisions, but that's not the way it works. That, in fact, our life on Earth includes opportunities to learn from our mistakes. We are here to learn, and often, for those in pain, quoting from Gibran, my favorite poet, 'To measure you by your smallest deed is to reckon the power of ocean by the frailty of its foam.' Many found the metaphor reassuring but, for some, their need to punish themselves was stronger than anything I could say. They had convinced themselves that daily recrimination and self-loathing were the hallmarks of true sincerity.

"This inability to forgive themselves made it very difficult for these women to forgive even the minor transgressions of others. How could they forgive anyone when they couldn't forgive themselves? They had created a prison for themselves, not realizing that the key to their cell was hidden in their hearts and could only be found by accepting their humanity—by giving up the illusion that if they are not perfect, they are not deserving of anything, especially love."

CB, fascinated by her work with the women, as well as her description of the glasses and asked, "How has your initiation changed you?"

Kathleen took a deep breath and didn't answer immediately. Her facial expression changed and she looked off into the distance, as if there was something there that would provide needed information. Finally, she looked down at the table and began to verbalize her thoughts.

"As part of my initiation ceremony I went on a vision quest that put me in touch with my past life. I learned that I am the reincarnation of Sappho's scribe. Sappho was a famous Greek poetess who started a school for girls when only boys were educated. She was a pioneer and considered by many to be the great-grandmother of the woman's movement. I learned that in my past life I wrote down everything she said and much of what she didn't say to others but told only to me. I was not only her scribe but her confidant, even though I was just a teenager. It was amazing. In the three years I spent with her, I learned more than many folks would learn in many lifetimes."

CB could not contain his curiosity and asked, "How did you get to be the scribe of Sappho? It doesn't sound like something you sign up for."

"It wasn't my idea. There is a world that exists outside of our world that we cannot see and that is just as real as this world. In some ways, it's more real because it doesn't contain many of the illusions we believe are true that aren't."

"For example?"

"Okay.... This table, for example, is not moving, right?

"Correct. It's stable."

"Wrong! Quantum physics tells us that everything is moving, even that which seems inert. If we looked at this table with a microscope that would allow us to see subatomic particles, we would see that everything is moving—and yet held together by an energy force that remains mysterious; a force that seems to hold everything together—the sun, moon, planets, and all universes—a force that we can't see."

"What does this have to do with becoming Sappho's scribe?"

"A decision was made long ago that in the twenty-first century our world would be headed towards chaos, war and catastrophe unless something was done on the human plane. I was a soul chosen to come to Earth to learn what I needed to know, so that, when I returned, I could be part of the answer to this multi-layered problem."

"Chosen by whom?"

"By the Ancient Ones. Those who have been here many times before and seen how power corrupts, and greed leads to cruelty, and cruelty breeds rage, and rage inspires war and destruction. I was sent here with a mission. You and I, as well as the women we have trained, are all part of the answer, I say 'part' because there is much more. But for now," she smiled, "I think I have answered your question."

CB chuckled, "You know, Kathleen, years ago I had a drinking problem and was involved in AA. If I told them this story at a meeting, somebody would be checking my meds and my sponsor would be calling me twice a day."

"I understand, but what I'm telling you is what I know to be the truth."

"Tell me more about your work with Sappho and how it helped you with the women."

"Back then, as it is now, women were not taught to express their feelings of anger. They were expected to deal silently with frustration, conflict, and unfairness and, in a sense, keep it to themselves. Of course, like today, they would discuss what was really going on with other females; however, the attitude that was expected was one of subservience. I learned from Sappho that this expectation is often the cause of depression and feelings of hopelessness. It's not so different today; girls, and later women, must learn that anger is a demon that must be faced and dealt with. Many women feel that if they express anger, they will not be loved and this fear often paralyzes them emotionally. Many of the women I spoke with had to learn that they have the same right as men to express anger and that in doing so, they felt a sense of power and freedom."

"This is fascinating!" CB stated.

"There's much more. For example, many of the women judged themselves far too harshly. They expected perfection from themselves—mentally, physically, financially, and personally. In other words, many tried to be all things to all people and needed to learn to say, no! Many women feel that if they don't do what others want, they won't be liked or loved. They give others power over them in the hope that they will be considered good or nice. It was the same way in Sappho's time and it is nonsense. But, I had to work with many of them on this recognition."

CB asked, "I know this is not related, but did you ever figure out how Coach and Star could read our thoughts?"

"No, but I did ask him before I left the ranch and he said he'd teach me during our next visit."

"I know we're scheduled to return there, but I haven't been given the date and time yet. Have you?

"No."

"Kathleen, I know the women were divided into seven groups of ten but I don't know what tasks they were assigned."

"Coach gave me the divisions during one of our walks at the ranch. They include: family, education, government, medicine, business, media, and environment. During their time at the hotel, and in our private discussions, I was able to identify the topic, or area of concern about which each woman felt passionate. Some had more than one area and, in those cases, I put them in the group that needed the fewest participants. I had learned from Sappho that we do our best when we are charged with a mission that we feel passionate about. So far, the feedback from the women about their group placement has been positive."

CB said, "I expect we'll hear from Coach in the near future so we can plan our next trip to the ranch. I'm very interested in how things went with the little girl chosen to assist us. As I understand, the plan is that she would be accompanied at the ranch by her mother and father. Apparently, Coach wants them to be involved in the process and be part of the team."

Kathleen said, "This is so unusual. A thirteen-year-old African-American gifted psychic who will travel the world with her diplomat parents and be able to provide us with information about the leaders in other countries in regard to their plans and trustworthiness. Wow, this is some team! And what is even more interesting is that we are being led by a man who most folks think is a myth or legend."

CB sat back. "Anything else we need to talk about Kathleen?"

Before she responded, the waitress stopped at their table and apologized for taking so long to get to them.

CB replied, "No apology necessary, we needed a few minutes to solve most of the world's major problems." He caught Kathleen's eye and they both smirked at the inside joke.

They ordered lunch and the discussion continued. "Yes! There is something that Coach told me that I need to share with you, and now is a good time. It is something quite extraordinary for a Buddhist monk."

CB eyed the waitress bringing over their cocktails and said, "Should I have the drink now, or should I wait to hear what you have to say?"

"You might want to start now and, by the time I finish, you might want to order another!"

"It's that kind of story?"

"Oh, yes!" she nodded. "From 1968 to 1970 the Blessed Virgin appeared over a Christian Coptic church in Cairo, Egypt. Prior to these appearances, which were witnessed by somewhere between five hundred thousand to a million people, crosses were placed on the doors of Christians signifying that they were to be executed. The apparition was first seen floating above the church and, during various appearances, the Blessed Virgin was viewed moving to various church sites as well as entering the church. It was witnessed by government officials, police, clergy, and the masses. It was widely reported in the newspapers and pictures were taken of the apparition. By the time the appearances stopped, no Christians had been killed."

"Is that true? Is that story real?"

"Very real! Everything Coach told me checked out. In fact, a number of miracles were associated with the visits: an elderly man was cured, a paralyzed man walked, and miraculously, a woman was visited by the Blessed Virgin and healed of breast cancer."

"You're right about that second drink! Tell me more."

"Coach told me to tell the women who are Christian to say the rosary every day for world peace and protection. He told me we are living in a very dangerous time and, in addition to our work, the need for divine intervention is the only answer that can save us from the forces of darkness."

When they had finished eating, CB and Kathleen exchanged phone numbers and email addresses and made plans for their continued work with the initiates.

"By the way," Kathleen asked, "remember that mysterious force that holds everything together that I spoke about?"

"Yeah, sure. The force that keeps what seems to be solid from flying off into oblivion."

"Many folks, including some brilliant scientists, think it's the love of the Creator."

Epilogue

by Zoey O'Toole

You might think that what Andy has presented here is farfetched: With nothing more than a few weeks' training, a group of spiritually minded women form a network with the intention of bringing the more traditionally feminine values of peace and love to a world that seems ever more focused on the traditionally masculine values of conquest and plunder. Never happen, right?

Wrong. It's already happening.

Women have been quietly taking advantage of the recent technological advances in communication to connect in non-traditional ways. As a society, "networking" has largely been the province of men, with the "old boys' network" being the backbone of political and financial structures of most western nations. Traditionally, women have been responsible for the home and children, which frequently took them out of public life and served to isolate them to at least some degree. Even today's "working" women – as if housework and childcare don't count as "work" – often take time off when their children are young, and, by the time they return to the job, have lost whatever networking advantage they may have had.

Recognizing the importance of networking to "climbing the corporate ladder," attempts have been made to create similar networks for women from scratch. Organizations such as The National Association for Female Executives sprouted up with the intention of leveling the playing field. While the goals and achievements of such organizations are admirable, they fall far short of actualizing the sort of network that most women seem to crave probably because they are focused on the same sort of goals that men's organizations have been focused on: climbing the corporate ladder in order to maximize profit for the stockholders and die with the most toys. A network based on those goals is never going to be truly satisfactory for the majority of women. Why? Perhaps because the majority of women become mothers. Women often leave public life – at least briefly – when they become mothers, and when they spend time outside the "rat race" many women find their values shifting or clarifying, leaving them feeling distinctly out of synch with our societal emphasis on "getting ahead."

William Ross Wallace said that "The hand that rocks the cradle is the hand that rules the world," but none of us are really fooled. No matter how much influence our mothers have had on our own personal lives, mothers have most assuredly *not* ruled the world. Until very recently, in fact, "ruling" was almost exclusively a male privilege. But in today's world, the landscape has changed. With the dawn of the Internet and, more lately, social media platforms that make networking so much easier than it has ever been before for people – all people – to connect on as deep a level as they choose, networking has already changed so much as to become unrecognizable to those who ran the networks of the past. Mothers of young children, one of the most traditionally isolated demographics – and arguably those most interested in making the world a better place for the small, vulnerable beings they are nurturing – are no longer cut off from the rest of the world. They now have the ability to interact with others to a degree that is unprecedented. And as a result, they are voicing their concerns and finding that many of them are shared by others.

One of the biggest concerns for mothers today is how to raise healthy children. Good health used to be considered a birthright, with chronic illness being an aberration. But, largely as a result of our society's emphasis on profit as the highest good, today's children do not enjoy the good health that most people enjoyed when I was growing up in the 1960s – back when we bathed the world in DDT, everyone smoked, there was no such thing as unleaded gas, and expectant mothers thought nothing of a cocktail or two. Today, one in forty-five children in the United States has autism; one in five has a developmental disability; one in five is obese; one in nine has ADHD; one in twelve has asthma; and one in thirteen has serious food allergies. Altogether, up to fifty-four percent of today's children are living life with a chronic illness, many of them taking one or more medications daily, many of those expected to be "for life." This situation has come about because we have allowed highly profitable corporations to consolidate our media, control the media's messaging through advertising dollars, and corrupt the governmental agencies charged with regulation of industry and safeguarding public health and the environment.

I belong to an organization whose main goal is helping children get – and stay – healthy; in other words, reclaiming our children's health from the corporate influences that have been undermining it. The Thinking Moms' Revolution began as a group of parents who found each other through social media and formed a bond around the health needs of our children that became increasingly important and valuable in each of our lives. Connecting with other parents on a regular basis enabled us to get questions answered reasonably well, reasonably quickly, and with a degree of humanity and humor not found elsewhere – all of which translated into better and cheaper outcomes for most of our children than we would otherwise have been capable of. Recognizing the value of this network, one member said, "We should write a book." None of us were really writers at the time, but we knew what we had was important, so we plunged ahead. Twenty-three women and one man contributed chapters, twenty-two of whom had children diagnosed with autism, many of them severely affected.

Once there was a book, we had to figure out how to sell it. We started a blog in February, 2012, so that people might get to know who we were and buy the book if we could ever get it published. When we began, we had absolutely no idea what we were doing. No one was in their comfort zone, but we did it anyway. We started a Facebook page to post our daily blogs, and it soon became clear that there was a clear need in the world for what we had, a network of people focused on giving and getting help to get and keep their children healthy. We quickly gathered a few thousand followers, sold our book to Skyhorse Publishing who published it in 2013, and then we went on to form a 501c (3) charitable organization (TEAM TMR) to help families offset the high cost of special-needs parenting. We published a cookbook and another book of autism stories written by a different group of moms who all donated their chapters to TEAM TMR, and we're close to releasing a book by and for grandparents of children with autism. We produce online webinars for very affordable prices (sometimes free) with cutting-edge healthcare practitioners we believe in who are getting exciting results.

We also became a part of the Autism Policy Reform Coalition in 2014 because we didn't think nearly enough was being done to address the huge increase in autism from a treatment, services, or prevention perspective. The APRC successfully lobbied Congress this year to allocate $26 million to the National Institute for Environmental Health Sciences to research environmental causes of autism, especially regressive autism. Through networking and talking one-on-one with thousands of parents over the past few years (our Facebook page is now very close to reaching 50,000 followers), we have found that specific environmental insults combined with specific genetic mutations and polymorphisms tend to be associated with allergies, asthma, ADHD, autism, seizure disorders, and autoimmune conditions. When enough of them combine early enough, autism is frequently the result. All of these conditions are for the most part avoidable and, sometimes at least, reversible, but you certainly couldn't tell by federal autism policy which has largely ignored the contribution that environmental toxins have played in the etiology of chronic conditions in today's children.

We recently launched TMR Nation, an Internet-based television network aimed at providing a repository of health-related information that is easily accessible to anyone who's interested.

Since we began the book that grew to become The Thinking Moms' Revolution, we have been operating continuously outside our own personal comfort zones, but in our collaboration and combined efforts we have found a new, much larger, comfort zone that we are constantly expanding. A number of us have been on television, met with members of Congress and state legislatures, or spoken at national conferences. Exciting as these things are, what we really live for are the heartfelt messages we receive every day from people who have learned from us, people who know that their children or grandchildren are far healthier than they might otherwise have been if they hadn't encountered our work. Those messages bring us to our knees and inspire a renewed dedication to continue despite the seemingly mountainous obstacles in our way. Margaret Mead was right when she said, "Never doubt that a small group of thoughtful, committed citizens can change the world; indeed it's the only thing that ever has."

And what we've kept first and foremost in mind as we do all this is that we do it for – and with – love. We've gotten a lot of pushback because we don't operate by the world's prime directive: "though shalt make as large a profit as possible." To many, we are seen as "dangerous" because we threaten the status quo. Fortunately, we are by no means alone. The organization, Moms Across America, has created a similar network of mothers specifically dedicated to taking back the food supply from the control of corporations such as Monsanto, whose pesticides and genetically modified organisms have become ubiquitous and difficult to escape. Senator Kirstin Gillibrand has been exhorting women to "get off the sidelines" and get involved in public life, especially politics, and has been providing virtual support and networking through a book club designed to inspire women to do exactly that. Glennon Doyle Melton created the Momastery website for "truth tellers & hope spreaders" and has brought together a large group of – again – mostly women who "belong to each other" by helping others in need. She recently co-founded a coalition formed to solve the Syrian refugee crisis. A wide variety of "mommy bloggers" are taking on similar topics all over the internet. Until recently, they have operated largely alone, but they too are finding that there is strength in connections forged with other like-minded people who are willing to take the lead from time to time.

I'm willing to bet that none of the women involved in these efforts felt like they were "ready" or had the training or background to lead a crusade or change the world – and yet that's exactly what we all find ourselves doing on a daily basis. Motivated by love – for ourselves, our families, and our planet – we find strength and empowerment in our combined efforts. And we are making the world a better place, one conversation at a time.

Join us and help create the world you want to live in.

Made in the USA
Coppell, TX
17 July 2020